ANSLEY CALLOWAY

Picking Peaches

First edition

This book was professionally typeset on Reedsy.
Find out more at reedsy.com

For those of us that want a sweet and easy love

Contents

1

Georgia

Tonight was the night that I decided to finally break my three year long dry spell of not getting laid. Keep in mind the dry spell was of my own choosing. Definitely not for lack of offers. My job gave me an incentive for jumping back in the pool of dating and hookups. Which might sound like a prostitution gig, but rest assured this was not that kind of job.

Lately I have been involved in a lot of jumping in blind. The only thing that seemed familiar in my life was my ever present anxiety about failing and the too many rings I wore. It was my own bright idea to move to a new town with new people while also tackling my new job all at the same time. New. The worst word on the planet.

My current new-to-me challenge was navigating this grocery store. Living in the same city all my life really hindered my skills for feeling comfortable in different settings. After walking up and down the medicine and vitamin aisles at least ten times each, I began to give up hope. The local Rosewood

1

grocery store was as organized as my junk drawer. And the prize package I required wasn't exactly the kind of thing I felt comfortable asking the geriatric aged attendant nearby about.

Aimlessly wandering about seemed like the best option in this scenario. So I started mapping out the store in my mind while walking down every long aisle. Toward the end of the soup aisle I noticed a brightly colored box in oddly familiar packaging. My legs carried me as fast as they could go without jogging.

As I reached out to grab it, a hand landed right on top of mine. A very large hand I might add. In shock, I snatched my hand away and snapped my head up to glare at the intruder. Physical touch was not something I often enjoyed from people I liked. Much less strangers.

"Oh sorry, did you need these?" A voice close to my ear asked, so I turned. Wow. He was hot and *very* tall. My brain couldn't even comprehend his words for a minute because it was too busy taking in his broad chest and strong shoulders. Which were way too close.

His fluffy blonde hair and dark eyes shone in the fluorescent lights of the grocery store. He stared down at me with interest and a little amusement. I was definitely staring and taking way too long to respond.

I snapped my head back to glare at the box of condoms while I tried to form words. His hand engulfed the entire package possessively. I insisted, "Yes actually, those are mine."

My eyes scoured the rest of the shelves and quickly concluded that this was the last box in the store. In the damn soup aisle. That was a new place for a box of condoms to be.

"Well actually, I believe they're in my cart so I'll be buying them. I sort of need these on short notice, but I hope you can find what you're looking for elsewhere, princess."

Did he just *pet-name* me? His smile shone so bright I damn near had to look away. So the thief is cocky too, how perfect. "I found them first. These condoms are going to be used in the next two hours so I would say that takes precedence over you restocking your supply."

"Twenty condoms in two hours, huh? You must have a real fun night planned." His dimples were showing now as one side of his lips turned up. Freaking dimples.

"Much more fun than this," I ground out. He may be hot but this was a matter of principle.

He rubbed the back of his head and looked down the aisle towards the registers. Any other night and I would have given in. Taken this as a sign tonight was best spent ordering in and rewatching a ten season TV show. But his arrogance was enough to turn my anxiety into anger. This hot angel man looming above me would not be the reason I didn't get laid tonight.

"What are you willing to do for them?" The offer was clearly a taunt. One I was totally going to fall for. At this rate my mind had one objective only; get the damn condoms. Nothing short of getting down on my knees and groveling was out of the question.

"What the hell do you want?"

"I could think of quite a few things, none of which are appropriate to say out loud in a grocery store." His smile hadn't faltered once, he was clearly enjoying making my cheeks turn pink out of anger.

"I'm sure your woman on short notice wouldn't appreciate that comment." My arms crossed as I stood my ground and blocked his exit towards the registers. "Unless you've paid good money for her company."

Sure Georgia, the best way to get a stranger to offer you kindness is to imply they've hired a prostitute. Clearly my mind was flustered by his presence still invading my space. Rather than getting angry, he only looked more amused as if he knew a secret I didn't.

"The only payment women receive from joining me in bed is pleasure. I can assure you money really isn't necessary for a woman to want to sleep with me." His eyes trailed up and down my body as if he was proving he could seduce me with just one glance. One thing the sadistic angel man did not account for was how stubborn I could be.

"As fun as this has been, I really have to get going." I pushed my open palm out and gestured for him to hand the box over. Of course, he didn't make any moves to reach for them in his basket.

So instead of arguing any more, I decided to take matters into my own hands. I scooped up the box. But as I was retrieving it, he stopped me with a hand on my wrist. "Persistent aren't you?" He lowered his voice and leaned in.

"Annoying aren't you? I found these first. They're mine!" His hand snatched them up and held the box over his head. I immediately stretched my arm as high as it could go and started to jump for it.

"Woah, woah, woah. Easy there, princess. Since you're so desperate, what if we share them?

"Yeah, again, no thanks. I won't be performing any favors for you." I huffed and backed up as he lowered the box again.

"Not like that. I mean what if I buy the box and give you some? That way we are both covered for tonight and our 'fun' plans." The offer seemed genuine as he tilted his head in

4

question. I supposed it was better than nothing.

"Deal." I swiftly turned and made my way toward the registers.

At least this way I got the condoms and saved some money. Angel-face trailed behind me and went through self check out relatively quickly. Not without throwing a few glances my way. I felt his eyes staring at my ass while I walked and became a little embarrassed about my unflattering jeans. All of my clothes were packed away so my wardrobe consisted of the crinkled t-shirts and jeans I packed in a backpack before moving.

Once we reached the exit after paying, he tore open the box and gave me five. "Will this be enough for your salacious event tonight?"

"No, I definitely need at least a few more." I kept my face even and gave him my best glare. If he was going to tease me, there was no way I was backing down now.

"Sure thing. Here you go then." He slapped down four more loose condoms into my hands. At this point I was struggling to hold them without dropping them all.

Angel-face walked backwards while waving at me and called, "Great meeting you! I really hope we can meet like this again soon."

I couldn't stop myself from watching him retreat to his car. Even the way he walked was self-assured. I had never met anyone with so much confidence in my life. He made sure to glance back at me and flash me his brightest smile. I slammed my car door shut and jammed the key into the ignition. My night could only go up from here.

2

Ashton

My encounter at the grocery store got me so worked up I was grateful Stacy reached out to hook up tonight. The fiery brunette that was prepared to maul me over a box of condoms interested me far more than I was willing to admit. Lately, my day to day life consisted of nothing but Uno and volleyball. I really needed to get laid.

The ride over to Stacy's apartment wasn't long. The last time we hooked up had been over five years ago, and she was still living in the same place downtown. That was one of the best and worst things about growing up in Rosewood, not much changed. She was probably still working at some diner downtown, or was she a bartender? The specifics didn't matter too much now I supposed. We were both just looking for a good time.

I shoved a couple of the condoms in my pocket after parking and jumped out of my truck. Multiple rounds seemed unlikely, but better safe than sorry. I unlocked my phone one last time to check in with my brother Nick before going in. He picked up immediately.

"Everything is great, now stop your worrying and go get laid." He hung up. Well that answers that I suppose.

My legs carried me up the steps two at a time until I reached Stacy's front door. It swung wide open at the first knock. She looked overly excited to see me. At least that was one woman tonight that wasn't burdened by my presence. "Hey, doll." I smiled.

"Ashton! It's been so long. We really should have done this sooner." She wrapped her arms around my neck and raised up to her tiptoes to kiss my cheek. My stomach twisted at the friendly greeting. I really wasn't interested in making any friends tonight, and definitely wasn't interested in leading her to believe I wanted a relationship.

Something about retiring and coming back to Rosewood made women think I was prepared to settle down and get married. Marriage was the last thing I was worried about. Which was one of the reasons I avoided any hookups for the last few years.

I pulled her arms down from around my neck and lowered my lips to her ear. "Should we head to your bedroom, or would you prefer I take you right here on the floor?"

That was more like it, less friendly, more douchey. I could play the role of manwhore easily. It felt much more safe to stick with that narrative than leave any room for questioning where this was going relationship wise.

"Why don't we start out on the couch?" She grabbed my hand and led me to sit down. Her knees sunk to the floor in front of me as she unceremoniously pulled a string on her top with one hand, uncovering her tits. My hand gravitated toward one as if magnetically attracted to it. It had been way too long since I'd done this.

I started pinching her nipple and unbuttoning my pants with my other hand. If she wanted to just kneel there while I jacked off I would consider this night a win. Tits are great.

That was when my phone started ringing. My body immediately tensed up and my hand left my pants to search the couch cushions where it must have fallen to. Her hand stopped mine and lifted it to her untouched breast before dropping her hands to pull at my pants. "Just let it ring, it's probably one of your friends inviting you out to a bar."

And trust me I tried to let it ring. I lasted fifteen seconds before I pushed her hands off of me and stood to yank up my pants. I snatched my phone and answered, "What's wrong?"

"She threw up." My brother answered, "I googled it and she doesn't have a fever so it's probably fine but she threw up and-"

My ass was flying out that door before he could finish the last sentence. While slamming the front door shut I turned to yell out a quick, "Sorry!"

I tore down the stairs and started up my car before peeling out of the parking lot. "Is anything else wrong, is she crying?"

"No, it woke her up but she seems okay. Her tummy hurts, that's all, probably because of all the peanut butter cups she ate before bed." He muttered the last part. Nick was out of his mind if he thought any of this was okay.

I took a deep breath as I turned down another street toward our home. "Why exactly were you giving her peanut butter cups before bed? I told you she could have a cookie and that's all!"

"She didn't want to get ready for bed so I was rewarding her for doing things like brushing her hair, putting on pajamas, and she even let me read her a bedtime story."

"Nick, she's not a damn dog. You can't just bribe her with treats so that she does what you want," I seethed. I loved my brother but God could he be an idiot sometimes. My fingers anxiously danced on the steering wheel.

"Look I'm almost home, I'm going to swing by the drug store and pick up some medicine just in case. I'll be there in five." I hung up before I heard anything else that could raise my heart rate.

Being a dad was the hardest job I had ever had in my entire life. I paced down the aisle of the drug store before finding the children's section. Ruth refused to drink anything other than the grape flavor, so I took an extra two minutes to shuffle through every box to find it. Victorious, I returned to the front, paid, and then raced back to my car.

While it wasn't easy, being a dad was also the best job I had ever had. After Ruth's mom left us in the dust three years ago the only way we survived was because of people like my brother. He and my other teammates from the volleyball league always helped out with anything we needed. The first time she ever walked was on a volleyball court. The boys and I all placed our bets on Ruth to be an Olympic volleyball champion one day.

I pulled up to my house and stalked up the front drive. The overgrown lawn stood out to me and I made a mental note to take care of it soon before summer was in full swing. I unlocked the bright red front door and speed walked to the living room where my brother sat with Ruth curled up in his lap. "Daddy!"

Her bright brown eyes looked glossy as she made grabby hands at me. I scooped her up from Nick's arms and turned her head up to me so I could get a good look. The back of my hand rested on her forehead to ensure that she didn't really have a fever. "You alright sunshine?"

"My tummy hurts." Her words were muffled as she buried her face in my shirt. I looked over her head at Nick who had guilt written all over his face.

I sat down on the couch next to him and rubbed Ruth's back while she nestled into my chest. Nick looked over at me. "So how was it?"

"How was what, asshole? The two minutes between you telling me she was okay and me racing over here?" I whispered back at him. My eyes raised to the ceiling as I blew out a breath. Honestly, I was sort of grateful my night got interrupted. As nice as it would have been to get laid, I much preferred my life as-is. Without any drama.

Nick stood up and walked back into the kitchen. I heard him rattling around in the cabinets before he walked back out with cleaning supplies and brushes. "I'm going to try to scrub it out of the carpet, hopefully it won't stain. It was mostly brown."

If anyone else offered to clean up my daughter's vomit I would shoot it down and spare them the trauma. But Nick was my twin brother and owed me ten times over for the gross shit he did when we were kids. He trudged up the stairs and I held Ruth until she fell asleep a few minutes later.

Twenty minutes passed before I walked through the door to Ruth's room and laid her down into her volleyball and princess themed bed. She insisted on having both when she turned five a few months ago. I kissed her cheek goodnight before glancing to the floor next to her bed. Nick had actually managed to get most of the stain out. I picked up some dirty towels and helped him carry everything back downstairs.

"Thanks for calling me man." I breathed out.

"Of course, I considered letting you have your night. But then I realized I wouldn't live to see the morning if I didn't tell you right away." I leaned against the kitchen counter before realizing the mess of dirty dishes in the sink was gone. The counters were clean too, even the overflowing trash can I had left was empty.

"Good call. I owe you one for cleaning up too. You should go home and get some beauty sleep, you're not looking as pretty lately as you usually do." His hand slapped my chest lazily for that one. He muttered in agreement and gathered his things before saying goodbye.

"And let me know how Ruthie is doing in the morning. I can take over for your practice tomorrow if you need to stay home with her." After promising to give updates and practically pushing him out of the door, I sighed and sunk down into my couch.

My mind wandered to the woman at the grocery store again, and I wondered if her fun plans tonight had gone any better than mine had. I fell asleep on my couch an hour later and woke up to Ruth poking my cheek.

3

Georgia

Birds chirping and bright morning light woke me up before my alarm. I laid in bed for a few extra minutes and relished in the fact that this was the last morning I would have to spend in this tiny hotel room. The clock told me that it was nearly eight in the morning by the time I managed to peep my eyes open and glance at it. I was going to be late if I didn't get my ass up and hurry to pack my belongings. My stuff was thrown across all surfaces of the hotel room.

Everything was tidy in thirty minutes and I checked out of the hotel. I typed in my brand new address to the GPS and was on my way. I made a quick stop halfway at the pet hotel my beloved companion was staying in until the house was ready. By the time we arrived, the service delivering my heavy furniture was due any minute. So, I moved my ring that looked the most wedding band-like to my ring finger after parking in the driveway. *My driveway.*

In the process of buying my very first home, I found that people (most of all men) didn't react well to a young woman buying a house on her own. So I had the whole married-but-he's-overseas routine down pat. A big truck pulled up behind me, perfect timing.

I hopped out of the car and got out my keyring to unlock the front door with a cat carrier in my opposite hand. I spent a few hours in my house here and there over the past few days to clean, but this was the first official day in my new home. It felt foreign and exciting all at the same time.

The large men moving my furniture introduced themselves and took no less than five minutes to ask for my husband. I signed the papers and kindly let them know that it would be just me today. Over the next hour they unloaded all of my heavy furniture much faster than I thought it would take. My giant writer's desk was the last piece to enter. On a whim I decided it should go in the sunroom right next to the biggest window in the house.

I made sure to tip them well and called my sister since I had to wait another hour for my giant moving container to be delivered.

To save money on moving costs, I rented a container to store the rest of my belongings. I accumulated a lot of stuff over the years of living with roommates. And when I decided to buy a house I went a little overboard on shopping for it. At least now I wouldn't need a storage unit anymore. Hopefully moving everything in alone wouldn't be too tricky.

She picked up relatively quickly and started, "So how is it living in paradise? Have you made new friends yet? Today is the big moving day, right? I can still drive down if you want help."

My older sister, Arden, regularly talked a million miles a minute. If sunshine was a person she would be it. She was also my older sister so it bothered me every time she was overly helpful. Especially when I knew she was working her ass off to achieve her dream of opening a bakery.

"I've been here for three days, of course I haven't made any friends. I haven't even met my neighbors yet." When Arden played twenty questions all at once, which was often, I typically picked only one to answer.

She chuckled at my non-cheery tone. "I really am more than happy to help if you want it. I asked for the weekend off even though you already told me no."

"I promise I am just fine on my own. I'm actually really excited to know every inch of this place." Which was true. Living with roommates or family my entire life, I had always wanted a place all to myself. And now I had it. "Plus you haven't had a weekend off in forever, you should go out and have fun."

My idea of fun and Arden's are quite opposite, just like our personalities. Her charm made her capable of making friends anywhere. I wouldn't be shocked if I got a call in a few days that she wound up on a free trip to Cabo with the hottest models and celebrities in Hollywood.

"Only if you insist. I want you to check in regularly though, it feels weird to not be able to run across the street and check on you whenever I want." She sighed. I knew she was worried about me. My anxious and introverted tendencies had only gotten worse over the last year. But this move was supposed to shake up my life and force me out of my comfort zone.

Honestly, this was the happiest I had been in a long time. Due to all of the recent changes, my career, love life, and sense of adventure were technically at an all time high.

"Wait, didn't you go out with a guy last night?! Why didn't

we start there? How was it?" Shit, I forgot that I mentioned that to her. The very last thing I wanted to talk about was my absolute disappointment of a one night stand.

I contemplated the best route to go with this question. "Oh Arden, I think the movers are here with my container. I actually have to go! Bye, I love you!" Click.

Hanging up on my sister was a cheap shot, but I had more important things to worry about today than my love life. Taking a quick nap before the movers arrived didn't sound like a bad idea. So I headed upstairs to sleep on my bare mattress, because I could.

The sound of a truck reversing into my driveway woke me up. I rolled out of bed and went to my bathroom to fix my bedhead before meeting the second set of movers. After signing some more papers, I was left with all of my belongings shoved into a metal box and no one to move them inside but myself.

The first hour was when I realized that I might have been in over my head. My arms were already beginning to get sore and there wasn't so much as a dent in the shipping container. Online forums told me that it was best to take more stuff rather than less and having to rebuy it all once settled into a new town. The internet never lies.

Around one I took a break and laid in the middle of my bare living room floor to catch my breath. The internet is bullshit. There was no way I would be able to unload that entire thing by myself in the next two days. I picked up my phone to google if I could pay extra to keep the container for longer. Maybe if I had a full week I could unload it all myself.

My break was short lived when the contract told me there were no extensions on renting containers. I had only two days

15

to unload all of my stuff. So my anxiety took over and I kicked into overdrive.

Two more hours later I was dripping in sweat and my arms were cramping from carrying so many heavy boxes. I set down the giant plant pot I was carrying and wiped off my forehead with the shoulder of my damp t-shirt. I took a second to sit on the top step of my porch to breathe. A giant black truck caught my attention as it pulled into the driveway next to mine.

The driver's side door swung open and a giant man stepped down out of it. He seemed to be distracted and quickly opened the door to the back seat. He leaned inside and pulled out a kid who he then set on the concrete. Distracted looking at the cute kid, I didn't even recognize him until he was fully facing me. No way.

My new hot neighbor is Angel-face. He didn't look my way, too focused on his very cute and very tiny kid. Wow, he had a kid. I wondered if that meant he also had a wife. The pair made their way inside and once the front door shut, I took that as my cue to keep working.

Around three in the afternoon I realized I hadn't eaten all day. Surely some food would replenish my energy and bring up my spirits. Moving absolutely sucked. I went into this expecting a fun day and quickly realized the amount of physical labor moving required.

I had just sat down at my kitchen table to eat my delivered Chinese food when my doorbell rang. The internet service installer wasn't due for another hour, but I supposed maybe he was early. I shoveled a bite of stir fry into my mouth before getting up to get the door.

A friendly smile was on my face to cover up the stress from this day. It quickly fell when I was met with none other than

Angel-face standing on my doorstep. I stood in shock, just staring at the pleased smile on his face. Did this man ever stop smiling?

I looked at his white t-shirt that was stretched out over those huge shoulders. I was pretty tall but this man standing in front of me was so tall my eyeline hit his collar bones. He was huge. Not to mention the lean muscles of his chest and arms made him appear even bigger than he was.

"Hello, neighbor," he cheerily sang. Movement behind his leg led me to look down and find the small girl he retrieved from the car earlier. She looked up at me suspiciously while holding onto her dad's leg.

My brain once again went rogue today and robotically replied, "Hello, it's so nice to meet you."

He smiled even wider and laughed under his breath. He sassily replied, "Right, because this is the first time we're meeting."

His hand reached out for the little girl and she took it as he pulled her forward, away from the cover of his leg. "We noticed you moving in and wanted to come say hi." He paused. "This little one here is Ruth and I'm Ashton. Are you moving in alone?"

His tone was still friendly and he glanced behind me as if hoping to see my fake husband appear out of thin air. He genuinely looked concerned. His gaze then fell to my hand which still had one of my rings moved to show I was married.

His face fell.

We shared a beat of silence before I reached to move the ring back to its normal spot. If he was my neighbor, he would realize there was no husband soon anyway. "I just put it there for the movers." He blew out a relieved breath.

I then put on my best fake smile and crouched down to be face to face with Ruth. She seemed wary so I spoke quietly, "It's very nice to meet you, I love your bracelet. Blue is my favorite color." I stood back up and added, "My name is Georgia."

Ruth just continued to stare at me. Pretty boy's pretty smile fell a little as he waited for me to reply to his original question. I straightened my shoulders and tried to speak with as much confidence as possible. "Oh and yes I am doing this alone. I have a few days to move everything though so I'm in no rush."

I awkwardly turned back toward the door, putting my hand on the handle. Hopefully he would take the hint that this fun little interaction was over. My stomach was aching with hunger now. His body turned away to look at the still practically full moving container and then he looked back at me. His face was skeptical. "You are planning on moving all of that alone?"

His eyes looked me up and down once again. I could see the cogs turning in his head and I did not appreciate it. I could barely handle my sister offering to help multiple times. This complete stranger offering was just insulting. Not to mention the fact that I had practically attacked him last night over a box of condoms.

"Yes, I am. Now if you'll excuse me I have some work to do."

I turned and walked through my front door before he interrupted. "Listen, I have some people that can help."

"No, thanks. Really, I have the money to pay for movers. I chose to do this myself."

He smirked and raised an eyebrow. Clearly this stranger had an affinity for arguing with people. "Give me thirty minutes and we'll come over to help."

My eyebrows furrowed in confusion. "No, really. I'm doing

this alone."

He flashed another playful smile at me and turned around without another word. Ruth grabbed his hand as he helped her down my front steps and I watched as they walked back to their house together. So much for not having crazy neighbors.

4

Ashton

Imagine my surprise when I looked out my front window and saw none other than my fiery brunette moving in next door. I had gone to sleep thinking about her and now my dreams were coming true. Her legs looked a mile long in those cut off shorts and her hair was pulled back in a ponytail that swung back and forth with every step. Ruth stuck her lollipop from the doctor's office in her mouth and climbed up on a chair to stare out the window with me.

"Who is that, daddy?" Her hand grabbed at my fingers.

The pretty girl next door was the only person I saw out there. Maybe whoever she was living with was busy doing something inside? She had made at least ten trips on her own in the last fifteen minutes though. Surely she would take a break soon. "She's our new neighbor, jelly bean."

I helped her down from the chair and we moved to the kitchen to get a snack. One great thing about my baby girl was that she loved to eat just as much as I did. I set her up at the table and continued to watch the girl outside work alone.

Ruth and I ate a snack, watched an episode of Bluey, and played a game of Uno. Each time I looked outside, she was still working alone. If my suspicions were right, I needed to go over there and help. One person moving an entire house alone was brutal.

From our interaction last night, something told me she would refuse the help anyway. But I had to at least try didn't I? Convincing Ruth to go over there with me wasn't easy, she still wasn't exactly fond of new people. A peanut butter cup did the trick, though I would never tell Nick about it.

* * *

That had gone about as well as I expected. At least I finally learned her name. *Georgia*. How goddamn pretty was that? I also got to see her cheeks turn pink again. Something about being able to make her blush made my heart race.

I pulled out my phone and posted a call for help in my volleyball league's group chat. Something about a damsel in distress trying to move an entire house on her own and needed help ASAP. This probably wasn't the best way to get on my neighbor's good side, but there was no way I was letting her move all of that on her own.

Within minutes a team of at least eight men had formed to help Georgia's cause. Now all I had to hope for was that she wouldn't slam the door in our faces.

* * *

Four cars pulled into my driveway as Ruth and I drew up our game plan in crayons. The 'game plan' mostly consisted of stick figure drawings of my team, but I was glad she wanted to participate. Once everyone had arrived we formed a huddle in the living room around Ruth's drawing while I gave the guys the low down.

"So, we need to move everything out of that shipping container," I pointed outside of the window. "Into her house in the next couple of hours."

"Sounds easy enough, we've moved houses before." Ryan looked suspicious. "But why exactly is the pep talk necessary?"

I debated my next sentence before speaking, "Well she doesn't want our help."

Eight different pairs of eyes deadpanned at me all at once. "So you want us to help a woman move against her will?"

"I mean that's technically stealing. Or breaking and entering. You're asking us to commit a felony." Man my friends sure could be dramatic.

I raised my hands in self-defense. "Pipe down, Stone. No need to be so dramatic." My eyes rolled as I helped up Ruth.

"We're just going over there to do a good deed for a pretty lady. Now everyone put on your best smiles and keep your heads held high." I led the troops out my front door as we marched over to Georgia's house.

I raised my hand to knock on her front door. But before my hand met the door it flew open. Someone walked right into my chest and I shifted a little to move Ruth out of the way. My free arm that wasn't holding Ruth's hand shot out to stabilize the person pushed up against my chest.

Georgia jumped back and shrieked at the contact. "You know we've really got to stop running into each other like this." I said with a grin.

She looked absolutely horrified, and her eyes continued to

widen as they shifted and she took in the team of tall men standing behind me. "Um, yeah. Did you need something?"

Nick stepped up and offered his best grin that could make nearly any woman chase after him. "We heard you were moving house alone. And turns out we need an extra workout this week, so we figure we could just kill two birds with one stone."

Georgia's eyes flitted from Nick to me and back again to Nick. Probably stressed out about the fact that there are two of us. Her head hung low to wipe sweat off of her chin with her shoulder. She let out a defeated sigh and then swung her front door open. She leaned down to shove a book in front of it as a door stopper.

"Knock yourselves out. What do you need from me?" At her approval, the rest of my team turned back to the open container and began grabbing boxes. With just Ruth, her and I standing on the porch I started to feel a little guilty.

"Are you sure this is alright? You can tell them to leave anytime and they will. But we really would like to help. Moving is hard enough, and no one should have to do it alone."

She glared at me with tired eyes. "I've been at it for the last four hours and I've barely made a dent. I'll pay all of you in whatever food you choose for dinner as thanks."

Ruth squeezed my hand and I looked down at her to check that she was good. I met Georgia's eyes again and felt less guilty knowing she completely exhausted herself trying to do it alone.

My smile returned, determined to get this job done. "Sounds great to me. Since you're in need of a well deserved break, do you mind if Ruth sits with you? She brought over her favorite coloring book and some crayons to pass the time."

Georgia looked alarmed again but still offered a hand to Ruth. My girl looked up at me in question. I handed over her coloring book and gave the crayons to Georgia. I gave Ruth a pat on the back which seemed to encourage her to start moving. They both walked into the house and I turned to start grabbing boxes.

* * *

Almost an hour later and we had made decent progress on unloading the container. Every trip I made involved checking in on Ruth and Georgia who sat at the kitchen table. They decided to color together. One side of the page was very neat and colored within the lines while the other was filled with scribbles of nearly every color in the rainbow.

Georgia remained quiet ever since the guys came to help. There were no more snarky comebacks from her. I wanted to bring that fire back, but seeing Ruth spend time with a woman other than Reese kept the smile on my face in place.

After the chaos of Ruth's mom leaving us, my kid developed trust issues around pretty much everyone except Nick and I. Even the guys on the team who she knew since she was a baby got the cold shoulder for over a year. Her therapist helped her make great strides, but strangers were still usually frowned upon by Ruth.

We tried out daycare a few months ago for the first time. She just turned five so it was time for her to start reading and learning, but it did not turn out well. The daycare called me up her second day and let me know it wasn't a good fit.

Thank God for my long time friend Reese Finch who happened to be a teacher. She and Ruth had weekly 'play

24

dates' which were more like fun tutoring sessions.

I set down the next box labeled kitchen. Georgia stood up and stopped me. "Hey, do you want me to go ahead and order dinner now?"

She looked uncomfortable, and I wondered if it was because of us barging in her house or her paying for the food. "I was just going to order some pizzas, you don't actually need to do that."

"Hell no, I want to pay. So let me buy dinner for everyone. Seriously, you've saved me a week's worth of manual labor." She scrunched her eyebrows up.

She leaned in and sarcastically added, "I also sort of owe you for yesterday."

I couldn't help the smirk from taking over my face. That must mean she was uncomfortable with us helping then. If paying would make her feel better, I'd allow it this one time.

"Okay, pizza's good then. Maybe some cheese and some pepperoni." I glanced around at Ryan and Clay who were standing near us. They both nodded and continued their work.

"I like pineapples," piped up Ruth.

Georgia turned to me and asked, "Ham and pineapple?"

"She likes pepperoni too, that will be just fine for her." I couldn't ask her to buy an entire extra pizza for my daughter's weird food taste.

Georgia nodded and asked me to sit with Ruth while she went to another room to make the pizza order. I sat down to admire the newly done drawing in her coloring book when I heard a screech.

"Tweet!" She screeched again. Footsteps sounded on the stairs as a cat darted out and Georgia followed soon after. Unsure of what to do I stood, but the cat slowed down and walked right up to Ruth. She giggled and petted its fur.

Georgia scooped up the fluffy black cat and apologized. "She's an escape artist, so I have to keep her in a closed room or she will think she's an outside cat."

I followed her to a spare bedroom and watched her set the cat inside and close the door. Georgia turned and stopped herself before running into my chest again. "You really don't owe me for yesterday." I said playfully.

She scoffed and rolled her eyes. "I know. I just don't like feeling indebted to cocky assholes." She cringed before correcting herself. "You're not an asshole. I appreciate you helping me move. You just act sort of-"

"Asshole-ish?" I offered.

Her smile widened. "You did try to steal my condoms."

Now it was my turn to roll my eyes. "I was nice enough to share them with you. Just let me know they didn't go to waste and we'll be even."

Her brow furrowed at my words. Then she blurted out, "Are you trying to ask about my sex life?"

"Well my plans sort of got trashed so I was hoping one of us was successful. Otherwise we caused all of that chaos over nothing." I couldn't keep the laughter out of my voice. Her fire was certainly back and she was pissed.

"Not that it's any of your business, but my plans were successful." Her arms were crossed now. She looked down at her feet with that angry little frown still on her face. She took a beat before finishing, "Sort of. It was kind of shit if I'm honest."

I couldn't stop the genuine laugh that loudly echoed throughout the empty house. What were the chances that two very hot people had shit luck with getting laid last night? My mind quickly went to ways I could turn her luck around.

Her sweaty shirt clinging to her tits did nothing but spur me on. Those cut off shorts showed off her pretty long legs and I wanted nothing but to throw them over my shoulders. And there was a very conveniently empty room right next to us.

Nope. My daughter was right in the kitchen. And getting with my neighbor was probably a very bad idea.

Georgia interrupted my thoughts before I could continue. "What happened with you? Ran out of money or something?"

I snorted. "No, my kid got sick. Her babysitter gave her one too many sweets."

That made her face relax. She glanced back to the kitchen where Ruth sat and nodded. "She's a sweet kid. And you're a good dad." She said it more to herself than to me.

I moved my body so it was no longer blocking her path and led us back to the kitchen. Sitting down next to Ruth I cheerfully announced, "Remind me to never get us a cat, sweet cheeks. I don't even want to know how that thing managed to open a door."

Ruth giggled again and turned back to her drawing. She started to get antsy in her chair and announced she was bored a few seconds later. I decided she should probably get out some energy before bed so we went outside and helped the others bring things in.

Our team worked quickly together, and with Ruth and Georgia joining in we had nearly all of it emptied by the time the pizza arrived. Everyone decided it was time for a break so we took over the living room with various mismatched seating around the wooden coffee table.

"Thank you guys again for helping me. I owe you so much more than pizza." Georgia said quietly while setting the boxes in the center of everyone. Plates were still packed away so paper plates and water bottles were passed around. The more time I spent with her around the guys I began to suspect that Georgia was shy.

I rested my hand on her shoulder and leaned in, "No problem, peach. Pizza is more than enough payment I can assure you. Stone over there was going to be eating dry bland chicken for dinner if you hadn't stepped in."

Clay rolled his eyes as most everyone chuckled at his lack of cooking skills. The man would take the flavor out of damn near any dish he touched. He was a local fireman and currently a part of our volleyball league. He used to be a pro but retired a couple of years back from an injury.

My attention went back to Georgia whose cheeks had turned pink once again. I relished in the fact I managed that twice in one day before I realized my arm was still lingering around her shoulders. I shifted away to grab a pizza box and set Ruth up at her seat on a pillow in front of the coffee table.

"Oh, I think the pineapple and ham is on the bottom." Georgia pointed out. I turned around and raised an eyebrow at her. Ruth clapped and cheered. She really did love food.

"Well Ruth was very helpful today too so it only seemed fair to get her favorite kind," she said quietly. Her lips turned up just a little and she bit her lip to hold back a smile. That was next on my list of achievements, making her smile would be the ultimate prize.

Dinner was eaten at record speed and we all went back to moving boxes while Ruth laid on the couch and watched Bluey on my phone. I stopped Georgia from reaching for one of the heaviest boxes and handed her a smaller one instead. She froze again at my hand on her elbow and slowly took the lighter box.

"I might have noodle arms but I can carry a box, you know," she breathed out. But she didn't move from my touch. I couldn't look away from her eyes, they were so bright and intriguing. Everytime our eyes met it was like I was drawn in, unaware of anything going on around us.

She shifted her gaze downward to the box so I pulled my hand back. "Take it easy please. I get you're a strong independent woman and all but there's no need to break your back."

That one earned me a quick laugh and an eye roll. How she managed to make an eye roll look sexy I will never know. My mind returned to my fantasy earlier as we both kept trudging through unloading the boxes.

After the last box was emptied most of the guys took a seat on the cold hardwood floor to catch their breath. I sat next to Ruth on the couch and let her cuddle up next to me. Stone was the first to leave. "It was great meeting you, Georgia. Welcome to town, I hope to see you around sometime. Maybe you can come to one of our practice matches or something."

She gave me a confused glance and painted on her cordial smile, "Yeah that would be nice, thank you so much again for helping out. You are all life savers. Literally."

Men piled out the door as they one by one told Georgia good night and she thanked them for coming. Then all that was left was Ruth, Nick, and I. We stood up to go and I started gathering Ruth's things.

"Practice matches? What does that mean?" I looked up at Georgia's confused face.

Nick glanced at me but I was once again distracted by those gorgeous eyes. My brain couldn't think while looking into those eyes. Nick answered her question for me. "We play volleyball. All the guys here tonight were from our league, most of them at some point played professionally but we all get together for fun now."

"Volleyball. I was thinking of soccer or baseball, but that answers a lot of my questions." She tapped at her full bottom lip. Looking at her lips proved to be even worse for my brain function. I tore my gaze away and finished picking up Ruth's crayons and book.

I couldn't help myself. I willed myself to have confidence and straightened my shoulders before speaking. "You really should come out sometime. It's a lot of fun, and Reese will finally have some company while we play."

Her head nodded and she sleepily blinked at me. "Okay, I'll think about it."

My smile returned in full force. "Great, well have a good night. I'm right next door if you need anything."

Nick shot me another glance as we walked towards my house. He muttered, "You are so damn obvious, you know that?"

I glared at him. There was nothing wrong with admiring my pretty neighbor. I wasn't looking for anything serious and he sure as hell didn't need to be the one to remind me of that. "Shut it, brother. No one asked for your opinion."

He laughed at my denial and leaned down to kiss Ruth on the cheek. "Goodnight Ruthie, I'm so glad you're feeling better today. Now we know, no more candy before bed huh?"

My little girl giggled and nodded. "Maybe just a little candy would be okay."

Nick and I shared a look while he repressed a shudder. Cleaning up last night must have been rough for him. He bid me goodbye as well and got in his car to go home. Ruth was in bed and asleep less than ten minutes later. I was up for far more than ten minutes thinking again about the girl next door.

5

Georgia

The first few days after moving flew by faster than I could blink. I did nothing but unpack, organize, and repeat. Tweet and I chowed down on food every morning and remained in the house until it was time to chow down on food again at night. My fenced in backyard made me feel comfortable enough to let her explore around after dinner before it got dark.

This morning was the first time I woke up to absolutely no boxes in sight. I stayed up far too late the night before breaking down boxes and shoving them into my overflowed trash bin. I scratched Tweet in greeting and headed downstairs after my morning routine. My desk called my name so I sat and loaded up my laptop.

Five days was the longest amount of time I had off work in a row in my entire adult life. Anxiety rushed through my body as I prepared to be overwhelmed with emails and notifications of 'emergencies' I missed while I was away. The little spinning loading screen seemed to take longer than ever before, as if it

5

was taunting me.

My anxiety was a little silly. Six months ago I quit my underpaid nine to five writing job for freelance writing social media content. In the last six months I made nearly quadruple the earnings of what I made during five years at the office job combined. I also really loved this job. My introverted nature held me back from making professional connections in the past, but I really do enjoy helping people.

My passion for writing stemmed from not having many friends in school so characters filled the role of my friend. Working for myself allowed me to help real people who grew platforms that spoke to thousands. My clients included 'influencers' that I really enjoyed. So I went from enjoying their content and personality myself, to helping them write that personality onto a page for others to enjoy. It was much more satisfying than writing for a corporation and not being sure if the words would ever even see the light of day.

Notifications came in as my laptop finally unlocked. I quickly skimmed going from oldest to newest. One titled as 'Book Deal !!' caught my attention. Reading thoroughly now, my eyebrows raised higher and higher as I went through the entire email. Holy shit. My newest client wants me to ghost write a book for her.

This was the same client that encouraged me to go out last night and hook up with nearly a complete stranger. She mentioned that she was working on a big project revolving around hook up culture. We shared our personal lives with each other regularly so she thought this would be the perfect excuse for me to get myself back out there. Her platform focused on giving advice about relationships and sex so I had to keep up to date on research.

A grin snuck its way onto my face as I audibly laughed. I read books nearly every day and yet I had given up hope that I would ever write one after middle school. A book! I stood up and scooped up Tweet into my arms to do a happy spin in my socks. A celebratory hot chocolate was definitely called for in this situation.

As I stirred in the mix with a goofy grin on my face, I heard a noise. I paused and realized it was the sound of my back door screen slowly opening. I didn't lock my back door because I rarely locked any doors. And if an intruder was going to break in surely they would be deterred by my cute wooden fence out back. Not.

I grabbed the nearest object that felt heavy, which was an empty pot sitting on the stove. Fully prepared to whack the intruder, I crept around the corner of my kitchen that led to the sun room. My crouch straightened when I caught sight of a very tiny human with a full head of blonde hair. "Ruth?"

Her head snapped up at me as she tripped and let go of the door. It slammed shut behind her and I rushed over to help her up. "Ruth, are you okay? What are you doing here?"

She shed a single tear and got up on her two feet. Consoling crying kids was not my specialty so I looked around helplessly and set the pot down on the floor. "Where's your dad Ruth?"

Her eyes wandered around my house before muttering, "Um, I wanted to see your titty."

Pause. I couldn't help the blatant confusion in my face as I backed up and laughed awkwardly. "You... you what?"

The determined look on her face scared me a little as she insisted. "Your titty I want to see your titty."

As if on cue, Tweet strolled into the room and walked right up to Ruth. If there was a time I would ever use the outdated phrase 'facepalm' this would be it. She just wanted to come see my cat.

I blew out a relieved laugh and squeezed my eyes shut to keep from laughing. Okay, maybe kids weren't all that bad. Ruth was pretty funny. I sat down next to her on the floor as she kept petting the cat. "Oh, you wanted to come say hi to my *kitty*! Sorry I misheard you."

She giggled as a fluffy tail swished around her face. We shared a quiet moment together admiring my cat before I realized something was missing out of this equation. "Wait Ruth, where is your dad? Are you alone?"

My head popped up as I looked out my back window in search of her much taller counterpart. She shook her head. "No, he's inside making eggs. He said I could go outside to blow on the dandelions."

I contemplated my options. "Ruth, do you like hot chocolate?"

She nodded her head quickly. I grabbed the pot that I planned on defending my life with and ran to the kitchen to make another cup of hot chocolate. I returned to Ruth and Tweet with two mugs in hand.

"Here, why don't we go sit outside and drink this? That way if your dad comes looking for you we can hear." She frowned down at the cat. "Oh, don't worry! Tweet can join us. She loves being outside."

She perked up at that and we headed outside. I didn't have any outside furniture yet so we sat on the steps while Tweet pranced around. I took the first sip of my celebration drink as we waited for Ruth's to cool off enough to be kid-temperature. I felt pretty proud of myself for remembering that much about children.

"Ruth!" Angel-face's frantic voice was audible all the way from his back door. I shot up and jogged over through the gate to wave at him. I caught his attention and was met with a very panicked Ashton.

He had very obviously just woken up with the blonde hair on the back of his head sticking in awkward directions. He even had pillow marks on his cheek. I couldn't help but glance down at his biceps framed by his tight athletic shirt. Even fresh out of sleep with bed head he looked hot as hell.

"Hey, Ruth is sitting with me in my backyard." I pointed over the fence. "She actually broke in through my back door. Smart kid, she wanted to come say hi to my cat."

He tore his gaze away and took long strides until he opened my gate and walked up to his daughter. I closed the gate behind us and watched as he stared down at Ruth letting out a long sigh.

He pinched the bridge of his nose and took a moment before speaking. "Sunshine, what did we say the rule was about staying in the backyard?"

Ruth's puppy dog eyes really were unmatched. She sweetly spoke, "Daddy I told you I wanted to see the kitty but maybe you didn't hear."

Wow this kid was going places. Not only did she have the puppy dog eyes down, but her argumentative skills were definitely solid too. Ashton bent down and stared for another minute. "Ruth, you can't leave the house alone. It's not safe."

She nodded. "Okay, daddy. I'm sorry." She pointed at Tweet and added. "I just really wanted to see the kitty again."

Ashton snorted and turned back to me. "Thank you for letting me know where she was."

"Anytime. We're having hot chocolate. Do you want one?"

36

I pointed to the mug sitting on the ledge near Ruth. "It's probably cooled off enough now, so you can drink it, Ruth."

Confused eyes stared into mine. "You do realize it's 65 degrees and almost summer right?"

I raised my chin and squinted my eyes at him. "I'll have you know hot chocolate is a delicious drink that can be had at any time of year. And I'm celebrating, which is all the more reason to have one today."

"What are we celebrating?" He smoothly lowered himself until he was sitting right next to the little girl on the porch. I rolled my eyes at his cheery smile.

I sat on the opposite side of Ruth and looked out over the yard. If I wasn't careful my goofy smile would take over my face again just at the thought of my new gig. "I got an offer to write a book, and someone wants to pay me to write it."

He held an imaginary glass and raised it to clink against mine. "Impressive. So you're a writer then. Our very own Hemmingway lives right next door. How about that, green bean?"

His arm slung over her shoulders and she did a slow blink. I imagined that was Ruth's version of an eye roll. Their comfortable relationship was incredibly endearing to watch. Growing up as a quiet kid, everyone kept their distance from me except for my sister. So it was sweet to watch Ruth and her dad interact without any awkwardness.

"Hey, do you know what time it is? I've been sort of distracted this morning." I tapped my phone and told him. He leapt off the step and raised a hand out to Ruth. "We're going to be late for weekend practice, sweet pea. We gotta go."

I took her half empty mug and stood up too. He smiled and thanked me again, "I owe you. Are you busy today? Maybe we can buy you ice cream later."

That sounded far too social and domestic for my liking. Sure, I wanted to branch out my social horizons in this new town. But I doubted I would make many friends at an ice cream shop with a hot man and cute kid accompanying me. "Sorry, book."

My brain clearly hadn't woken up enough yet. He smirked anyway. "Right, book. Good luck with that, peach. Nice to see you." And just like that I was left alone again.

6

Ashton

Ruth and I headed to the car to go to weekend practice with tiny shoes and socks crumpled in my left hand. I turned around in my seat at the red lights to hand her the socks and shoes one at a time to slip on her feet. Once in the parking lot I tied the laces on her left shoe while Ruth insisted on tying her right. I unbuckled her and helped her climb to the ground once she finished. "I'll race you!"

I couldn't help but smile and follow after my girl. I let her win the race and swung her into the air as we walked through the doors of the gym. Her squeals of glee announced our arrival. Reese headed over with Ryan trailing close behind her. "Wow, Ryan Summers; star player of the Gold Giants graces us with his presence? Careful, I might just get nervous."

A well-deserved slap landed on my shoulder. He rolled his eyes and hovered over Reese's shoulder. "I'm home for the weekend."

"Well I hope you're stretched because we're doing passing drills and death sprints today." I leaned down to kiss Ruth on the cheek. I greeted Reese and promised to buy her lunch for staying with Ruth before handing over Ruth's bag. "Come on Summers, let's get moving."

My gym bag tossed to the side, I walked over to the rest of the guys already talking in a huddle. Nick and Will seemed really intense for the start of practice. I cleared my throat and waited to hear whatever it was they were arguing about. Both my brother and Will Rose were quiet types, but when they had an opinion there was no changing it.

Will spoke first. "We need a coach for the charity match."

My eyebrows rose. "Charity match?"

Clay Stone, our local fire fighting hero stepped in. "Some old pro buddies of mine put together a team. They want us to put together our own and play for a crowd a month and a half from now. The only rules are no current pros."

"One of us needs to be the coach for it. I think Will is the most level headed." Nick added.

Will glared openly. "Any of you assholes ever asked me for a pep talk?" He looked around at each one of us. "That settles that."

I thought about who would be a good leader and my eyes immediately landed on my brother. "It's gotta be Nick then. How about we put it to a vote?"

Hours later I collapsed on a bench and gulped down an entire bottle of water. We practiced in an open gym and occasionally on the beach for fun. So people sitting on the sidelines to watch wasn't out of the ordinary. But today we had quite a lot of visitors. I felt eyes on me as I walked up the stands to Ruth.

"Hey, honey bun. How are we doing up here?" Ruth looked up from her coloring book and smiled.

"I colored a princess. But Ryan told me I colored it wrong."

6

I looked down at the page and saw a princess colored in with blue hair and green skin. Then my head turned to Ryan who tapped out of practice early and skulked back to Reese's side about an hour ago.

"Well what the hell is wrong with it Summers?" I accused. He raised his hands and rested an arm behind Reese.

"Nothing, all I said is I'd never seen a princess with green skin before. It looks great."

"That's right, it's the prettiest drawing I've ever seen. We should put it on the fridge when we get home." I pinched Ruth's cheek and she giggled. She absolutely loved tattling on our friends and seeing them get in trouble with me.

Reese leaned in and shifted her eyes, suggesting I look at the opposite side of the gym. My eyes followed her and landed on a familiar blonde. "Stacy Richards has been here for almost the entire practice. She does not look happy and hasn't taken her eyes off of you, any idea why?"

My body flooded with guilt. I hadn't even had a second thought about her since I ran out of her apartment that night like my pants were on fire. I should probably go over there and apologize. But she really did look angry and I did not want to cause any sort of scene in front of Ruth.

Summers laughed at my obvious discomfort. "Well I guess that answers that."

"Why don't I go get lunch while they run through this next match? Ruth, do you wanna come?" I asked. Maybe if I left the building Stacy would take the hint and leave too. I would have been more than happy to explain and apologize but not in public and in front of my daughter.

She stood up happily and took my hand. Reese straightened in her seat and spoke eagerly, "I have been craving Mexican

41

food for days. Can we do Lucky's?"

Ruth and Ryan both went along with the plan. I got Reese and Summer's orders and we were on our merry way. It took about thirty minutes in total to drive down the street and pick up food for the four of us before arriving back at practice.

I dropped Ruth and the food off at the stands. Unfortunately Stacy didn't take the hint and stopped me on my way back to the gym floor. "Hey, nice to see you again."

She did not look or say that greeting nicely. I cringed and tried to offer a smile. Thankfully Ruth was out of earshot but Nick and Will were sitting on the bench nearest to us. "Stacy, I've been meaning to call you. I'm so sorry about the other night but my daughter got sick and I needed to take care of her."

Her face did not seem to buy the sick kid excuse. I heard a snicker behind me and had the urge to spin around and slap my brother on the back of the head. Stacy spoke angrily, "Right, well let's not do it again. Have a nice life."

Stacy stormed off and what I assumed were her friends fell into formation behind her as she exited the gym. This had to be a new low. I somehow inspired enough hatred for her to go out of her way to tell me to fuck off. I honestly only remembered getting the call that Ruth was sick and blacked out until I got home. Hook ups probably weren't the best move for me yet.

Nick's face looked very amused as I sat down next to Will. "Fuck off."

Will looked pained at the awkward interaction. Neither socializing nor women were his area of expertise so if even he was judging it was worse than I thought. "What the hell did you do to her? Stacy was one of the few people in high school that didn't torture me."

"It was a misunderstanding, we were about to hook up and then Nick called that Ruth was sick and well, I ran and didn't look back." I muttered while retying my shoelaces. He cringed even harder.

"How's your new neighbor?" Nick had asked me several times over the past few days about Georgia. He was not going to let that ship sail.

Will looked between our staring contest. "Is that the one that the SOS was for? I was working late, sorry."

"Ruth broke into her house this morning. Apparently I fell asleep after breakfast and she decided to go pay Georgia a visit." Their eyebrows both rose sky high. My life had been feeling a little dream-like lately. I wonder if I fell into an alternate universe.

Nick called Clay over and they all spent a few minutes quizzing me about the interaction. My brother was smiling like he knew something I didn't by the end of it. A whistle sounded and it was our turn to play again.

After practice Ruth insisted on picking up a milkshake on the way home. I didn't like giving her a lot of sugar in one go after the throw-up incident but we stopped for a vanilla milkshake with no cherry anyways. My truck pulled into the drive slowly or else Ruth would make her 'Daddy don't run into the house again' comment. I tapped the garage door once and almost a year later she hadn't forgotten it.

As I was grabbing my now cold Mexican food from the back seat I saw Georgia pull in. I made sure to take longer unbuckling Ruth to be able to say hi. When my body uncrouched from the truck I was met with the sight of Georgia struggling to carry far too many grocery bags in one go.

Hand in hand my daughter and I wordlessly walked up to my neighbor. I called, "Hey, peach. Need some help there?"

She grimaced and lifted her arm that was overflowing with plastic bags. "That would be helpful if you don't mind."

"Hand them over." I took her entire right arm's worth and waited for her to grab her keys before trudging up the steps to her door.

We walked in and followed Georgia to her kitchen. The big windows in this house really opened up the place. It was a beautiful house and now that she had furniture in it, the place felt even more homely. "So what is all of this for exactly?"

Now that I looked around more I spotted what I assumed was flour or sugar sprinkled across the island in the middle of the room. And also plates of cookies on the table in the corner. Ruth saw them about a half a second after I did. She squealed, "Cookies!"

Georgia laughed. "I'm stress-baking while I come up with ideas for how I want to write the book. My client is mostly giving me free reign on how to do this. Some people get good ideas while in the shower. I bake when I need ideas or to solve a problem." It sounded like she had explained this before. Georgia looked over at Ruth and offered, "She's more than welcome to have some if that's okay. I have far too many."

I quickly shook my head and lifted the groceries onto the island. Then I raised the half empty milkshake in my other hand. "She just had a milkshake so we are all full on sugar." I said pointedly at Ruth.

"But daddy I haven't finished it yet. And Georgia said it was okay. She tugged on my arm and flashed those puppy dog eyes. I sighed.

My eyes met Georgia's again to make sure it was really okay.

44

She nodded again and smiled before insisting, "Really, please take some home too. I have more than I know what to do with. And I don't know anyone here so it's not like my friends will come knocking down the door for some."

I grabbed one for Ruth and one to try myself. Ruth scarfed it down at record speed and my growling stomach encouraged me to go for a bite. Practice had been long and tiring. And my stomach was punishing me for not eating enough at breakfast.

My mouth froze as I took the first bite. My teeth crunched into the cookie and I had to rip the cookie apart to finish chewing. A distinct burnt taste hit my tongue. I forced my face to keep the smile I had before and finish chewing slowly before swallowing. "Wow, those are great! Thank you."

"Really? My sister is a baker, her stuff is absolutely amazing. I mostly just bake out of stress so it doesn't always turn out well." Georgia explained. Bags of flour and sugar were unbagged and stacked on the counter. "I'm going to make brownies next. Maybe I could bring some over for you to try! My brownies are probably the only thing that turn out edible regularly."

She sounded so happy that I was able to choke down her cookie. There was no way I was going to do anything to jeopardize that smile.

I let the excitement I felt to see her again bleed into my voice. "I would love that. Brownies are my favorite. And I'm sure Ruth will be stoked as well for a reason to have more sugar."

We bid our goodbyes and I hurried to our house to gulp down an entire glass of water. I dug into my cold Mexican food quickly. Then Ruth and I spent the rest of the day cleaning up the house and playing with her stuffed animals.

7

Georgia

The first half of my day was spent emailing back and forth about the book proposal. One month and a few days was all I had to write a full 200 page book on 'Relationships and Hookup Culture'. How hilariously ironic is that? At least I had spent the last few months researching relationships to write for my clients blog. I felt pretty confident in my abilities.

So did my client apparently, because she was explicit in letting me know that she trusted me to do my best work. I offered to do check-ins with her each week to go over my progress. But she insisted I knew best and she would review it once everything was finished.

Beeping sounded from the oven as I finished jotting down a few more chapter titles for potential topics to cover. I spun around and popped the oven door open to check on the tarts. They looked golden-y brown to me so onto the counter they went. Various treats now covered nearly the entire kitchen island.

Ashton's words came back to my mind and I remembered that I was supposed to bring over the brownies after they were finished. Shit. I rushed to wash my hands and pulled the strings undone from my apron, returning the pink fabric to its hook. Dish in hand, I shrugged on a hoodie and hurried out the door.

My walk was illuminated by streetlights as I headed over and knocked twice. I was greeted by a confused look on Ashton's face. Maybe he forgot I was coming. I hesitantly spoke, "Hey, I brought the brownies."

It had been a while since I spent time with anyone but my sister. A nagging feeling made me think something was off. Did he not mean it when he said I should bring brownies over later? And then I looked down at what he was wearing. Pajama pants and a crumpled t-shirt. Then I took in his slightly mussed hair.

"What time is it? Were you sleeping? Oh my god I am so sorry!" I backed up and began to turn to flee back to the safety of my house when he grabbed my arm.

"Easy, peach. It's okay, come on in." His arm beckoned me inside. I hesitated and he insisted. "Really, it's okay. I was just watching a shitty TV show. This is a welcome distraction."

I stepped inside slowly. His house was nice. All of the furniture looked very simple and clean, but there were definitely traces of Ruth on nearly every surface. Loose crayons left on the coffee table, tiny pink shoes next to the door, and fairy wings hanging on the wall were some of my favorites.

"I really am sorry for coming over so late. I lost track of time while I was baking." I followed him to the kitchen and admired the view of his broad back and narrow waist.

He grabbed plates and turned so I could see his smile. "I

really don't mind. I was just surprised." He reached out to take the brownie dish and began slicing pieces.

I distracted myself by wandering off a little and looking at the pictures hung on the wall. Lots of Ruth baby pictures smiled back at me. There were also a bunch of what I guessed were volleyball team pictures, and even one of what I thought was baby Ashton and his twin brother.

A hand rested on my shoulder as he offered a dish with a brownie on it. "She's a cute kid huh?" Pride and admiration took up every inch of his face.

"She's a great kid. And hilarious too. You're lucky to have her." Choking on the brownie, I recalled her mispronunciation earlier that morning. My head turned to see Ashton take his first bite too. He seemed hesitant at first and I worried that maybe he was lying earlier about liking the cookies. Relief lit up his face as he nodded and hummed.

"They're good brownies, thanks for sharing." He breathed out. I let out a quiet laugh and moved to sit down at the kitchen table.

"So you and your brother have played volleyball since you were little?" He nodded and took a swig of milk. "I always wished I stuck with a sport. I was never great at anything I tried, so I always gave up pretty early on."

"You don't just pick up a volleyball and start playing in the pros. It takes time, pretty much every sport requires years of practice until you're any good." He softly explained.

His empty plate stared back at me. "Just like baking I suppose." I snarked and laughed as the look on his face confirmed how guilty he felt for not liking the cookie earlier. "I'll make sure to throw those cookies out so I don't harm any future well-intentioned neighbors."

7

Nervous laughter rang throughout the kitchen. "I really don't mean to hurt your feelings. They just weren't my cup of tea." I made a mental note to try one when I got back home.

"So you played pro? Does that mean you don't anymore?"

"No, when Ruth's mom left us I decided it was best if I stayed close to home. It required a lot of traveling and that's not easy to do alone with a two year old." He paused. "That's okay though, I ended my career on a high note."

Asking about his ex-something seemed too personal so I started with the easy stuff. "Did you win a tournament or something?"

He laughed. "I didn't win, but we did get to play in the 2020 Olympics. That's one of the best ways I could have imagined going out."

My forehead crinkled in surprise. "The Olympics? As in capital O the Olympics?"

A handsome smile took over his face again. "What, are you trying to question my skills?"

I shook my head and joined in on his laugh. My head rose in defiance. "Well I've never seen you play so how should I know?"

"We'll have to change that then." His eyes were determined and excitement filled my stomach at the thought of seeing him play.

The next few hours involved nearly every subject under the sun. Volleyball talk turned into discussing my baking skills which led to talking about my sister and then his brother.

I learned that he was twenty eight and he was shocked that I just turned twenty six. He mentioned that Ruth's mom left them for another man after finding out she was pregnant with someone else's baby. That was quite a bomb drop.

49

He insisted it was ancient history and not a big deal. So I changed the subject. "If you don't see me for the next few days, just know I'll be hunched over at my desk typing away for hours non stop. I've never written a full book before, but I go for days on end already when I have articles all due at the same time."

His arm slouched over the table rose to stretch over the back of his head. He yawned, "I'll have to do a few check-ins to make sure you're still alive in there."

The thought of Ashton caring about if I lived or died made me blush. The bar is so low in hell. "Be careful, I might hiss if the sunlight touches me."

The joke was dumb but he laughed at it anyway. "So what websites do you write these articles for?"

"Oh, nothing you've ever heard of. They're blogs of people who specialize in different industries, Kale Me Cooked is the one about health foods. Sandy Feet travels the world so I get to write about the fun cities she's been to. And there's a plant blog that lets me write all about different kinds of house plants called Pothos and Vine. That one is probably my favorite.

Realizing I rambled on for too long yet again, I looked over at the clock. My seat nearly tipped over as I backed up and stood too quickly. "Holy shit, it's already one a.m. When did I get here?"

"Just after eleven, but that's okay. You're awfully jumpy, you know." He stood with me and walked me to the door.

I turned to say goodbye but he just motioned for me to keep walking all of the way out the door. We walked side by side back to my side of the yard. He spoke quietly, "I really am glad you came by. And I absolutely will be checking up on you. Try not to work yourself too hard."

50

My cheeks once again betrayed me as I blushed. "This was surprisingly nice. Enjoy the brownies and have a good night." I forced myself not to turn back around as I closed the door. We were neighbors, not some high school kids giddy over talking in the hallway after class.

The lights in the kitchen caught my eye so I made my way to turn them off. Then I remembered the cookie debacle. I really should try one if Ashton felt so bad about not liking them. Tweet settled at my feet as I raised one to my lips. The cookie crunched around my teeth and my face squished together in disgust. I cannot believe I made him eat this. They were so burnt.

Pushing the embarrassment of those pitiful cookies into the back of my mind, I headed upstairs to get ready for bed. Once I was cozy in bed with clean teeth and brushed hair I pulled out my phone. Then a thought struck me. A quick YouTube search showed footage from the USA Olympic team and after a few minutes of scrolling I finally found a familiar face.

8

Ashton

The clock read four a.m. as I finished reading the tenth blog post on Pothos and Vine's website. Never in my life had I cared to know about plant care and the different varegations plants could have, but Georgia's words drew me in. I started out a few hours ago only planning on skimming a few of her articles to see her writing.

Georgia walked into my life like a whirlwind. Now that I had gotten close to her I was swept up in her pretty words and even prettier eyes. Even after spending hours talking to her and then reading her work I was still left wanting more.

I returned my phone to its place on the bedside table. The ceiling of my bedroom taunted me as my brain told my eyes to close and go to sleep. There were at least four more blog posts of Georgia's that I could be reading right now. My morning would be filled with regret if I did though. Ruth was an early riser.

Something wet poked my cheek and I flinched out of sleep.

My foggy eyes blinked away the restful few hours of sleep I got and landed on my daughter standing next to my bed. In her hand was a purple marker. Instinctively I closed my eyes and pretended to lay back down. Little girl giggles kept me awake though.

I caught the hand going in for my cheek again and she giggled even more. "Daddy you look so pretty!"

"Ruth, what are you drawing on my face?" I asked sternly. She stifled her giggles because her full name meant it was serious.

"I wanted to give you freckles to see if they make you prettier. I want freckles. I asked Reese what they were on her cheeks and Ryan said that freckles make you pretty."

I squeezed my eyes shut tight. If Summers was the reason I woke up with purple marker all over my face he was totally getting his ass handed to him before he left town again. I sighed, "Thank you, butter cup. Why don't we go see how it looks?"

Rolling out of bed, I scooped up Ruth on my way and carried her over my shoulder to the bathroom mirror. The giggles returned in full. My face fell as I took in the sight of my new freckles. My hand rose to my jaw and rubbed. Definitely going to need more than water to get this off.

"Well they certainly are colorful aren't they?" I set Ruth down on the counter, grabbed my face wash that wasn't used often enough, and began scrubbing.

Twenty minutes and a very red face later, I decided my face was as good as it was going to get. I helped Ruth hop down and got us both ready for the day. My kitchen welcomed me with an empty fridge and slim pickings in the pantry. "How about we go see Uncle Nick for breakfast?"

I took the screech that followed as a yes. One short car ride and we were walking into Reid's Diner hand in hand. The look my brother gave me as he took me in told me that I hadn't washed my face as well as I thought I had.

"What happened to you? You look like you're having an allergic reaction." We sat down at the stools in front of his bar. I rolled my eyes and set Ruth on top of her own stool.

"Someone decided to make me prettier this morning. What do you think?" I batted my eyelashes with my best princess smile.

Nick looked back to Ruth with a lifted eyebrow which earned a few more giggles. "I gave daddy purple freckles! He's not pretty anymore though because he washed them off."

"Ah, I see. Permanent marker?"

"Clearly." I said shortly. Nick snorted and rolled his eyes.

He leisurely stood and walked around the counter. "So what does my favorite person on the planet want for breakfast?"

"Pancakes." I answered, very aware that his favorite person was the one sitting next to me.

Ruth giggled and Nick took off his hat to slap my arm with it. "Ruthie, how about some french toast? I have some fresh strawberries and I'll cut them up into the little hearts how you like?"

A very happy little girl nodded. "And I want a flower one too." I shot her a look. "Please."

"Alright, coming right up. And I'll throw in some pancakes too for Pinkie Pie over there." His head tilted toward me. I pulled out my phone camera to check out how bad my face really looked. Somehow in the lighting of the restaurant I looked even worse than my bathroom.

The doorbell chimed and I turned as I heard familiar voices.

What a surprise, Ryan Summers must be one lucky bastard to walk in right now.

"Hey, Summers. Come over here for a minute." Ruth eagerly sat up close to the counter and waited for a fight. My girl was going to love reality TV when she grew up.

Ryan strolled up and sat down next to me. "What happened to your face?"

I slapped my arm across his back and wrapped it around his neck to pull him in close. "Well turns out Ruth here learned about freckles yesterday."

"Freckles?" A corner of his lip turned up. He must have known where this was going.

"Yeah, someone told her they're pretty. So she wanted to try putting some purple ones on me to see if it was true." Nick walked up and shot me a look.

"Please try not to kill anyone in my diner."

I squeezed Ryan's neck a little tighter and let him go. "So this is the aftermath of what's left on my face."

Reese walked in soon after and sat down hurriedly. "I'm starving, so I'm stealing a muffin. I can't wait but I'll pay."

"So did you look pretty Ash? Purple *is* your color." He smirked. Ryan Summers must have a death wish. Ruth burst out into giggles again.

"Yeah, they turned out great. Hey Ruth, how about you give Ryan a makeover next? You can try out rainbow freckles. And maybe fix that long hair of his that's always hanging in his face. I really don't know how you play with that hair."

Ruth grabbed my hand. "Maybe we could braid it for him, daddy. He can wear it like that for his next game." That got a smile back on my face.

"What a great idea, pop tart. I think we should." Ryan rolled his eyes and Reese pulled away from her ginormous muffin enough to laugh.

Seeing Reese eat a muffin reminded me of Georgia telling me about the 'Poppyseed Muffin Fiasco of 2013' last night. I decided at that moment to buy her coffee on the way home for her first day of writing. Last night I also learned she liked her latte with two sugars because that was the way her sister drank it when Georgia was envious and still too young to have coffee.

In the drive thru Ruth asked if this place sold milkshakes. "Ruth it's nine in the morning. And Uncle Nick just gave you a mountain of whipped cream on top of your french toast."

"But Daddy, that was for breakfast. I want a treat," She begged. I tried my best to keep my eyes from rolling.

"Georgia left us some brownies at the house. Do you want to have one of those after lunch today?" I countered. The past few years have taught me that parenting is a lot like constantly negotiating with a haggler. I hoped my counter offer was good enough to accept.

She nodded and kicked my chair for good measure. "If Georgia made it, it must be good." I really needed to get her taste buds checked if she had the nerve to make that statement after having one of Georgia's cookies yesterday.

"Okay so Georgia is writing her book today and I was thinking we could play a prank on her." Georgia made it clear yesterday that she didn't want to be disturbed too much. So I didn't want to make a thing out of this and barge in less than twelve hours after we last saw each other.

"A prank? I'm good at jokes and pranks are kind of like jokes right?" She kicked my seat again.

"Exactly. I was thinking I could teach you some ding dong

56

ditch skills." She tilted her head like a confused puppy dog.

In the driveway, we stayed quiet and sneakily stalked over to Georgia's front door. Ruth let out a few giggles from excitement. I pretended to be scared and hovered my hand over her mouth. She began to laugh even harder. I placed the latte down on the doormat and asked Ruth if she was ready. Her head bobbed quickly.

My hand lifted to the doorbell and I whisper-shouted "Run!" to give her a head start. Ruth ran off loudly belly laughing now, I gave her a few seconds head start before ringing the doorbell and chasing after her. We safely made it to our door and peeked around to make sure the coast was clear before heading inside.

* * *

Two days later I stood on Georgia's doorstep again with Ruth. Every morning we made sure to leave her coffee and breakfast before ding dong ditching. This morning I worked up the nerve to invite her to practice later. Her car parked in the same place told me she hadn't left her house for nearly three days. I was beginning to get worried about her isolating herself. She did warn me, but I didn't expect her to literally only write all day every day.

Plus I wanted Georgia to leave her house for my own selfish reasons. I could not stop thinking about her. I wanted to know how her writing was going. I wanted to know if she was taking care of herself and getting fresh air. Most importantly, I wanted to know if she thought about me too.

Two knocks later and our feet stayed firmly in place on the doormat. Ruth squeezed my hand and Georgia greeted us with sleepy eyes and bed head. Her usually silky smooth hair was piled on her head in a very messy bun with flyaways pointing in every direction. The big t-shirt she wore hung over her tall slender frame. It was so big I was left wondering if she wore shorts under it. Her smile made my heart race.

"Good morning, sleeping beauty." So cheesy, but I couldn't help myself. The peachy pink color on her cheeks again was better than any sunrise. "We brought you breakfast, but we also have a proposal for you."

She popped her hip and leaned against the doorframe with her arms crossed. I missed that sarcastic attitude so much while we were apart. "I'm listening."

Ruth took over for me and stammered, "Daddy has to coach later. And it's really boring when he coaches because I have to sit alone and watch. But it could be fun if you came and colored with me again." My baby girl knew how to really sell it.

Georgia uncrossed her arms to twist one of her rings. I wanted to ask why she wore so many. Did they all have some special meaning? Each one seemed to be different, maybe one day- nope. What the hell was wrong with me? Marriage was the last thing I wanted.

I started talking, if only to distract myself from my own thoughts. "I know you're writing, but it could be nice to get some fresh air. Help your brain recharge from all those big words you're using."

"How long does practice go for?" She asked hesitantly.

"Usually only an hour and a half. I just coach high school kids over at the school. Maybe two if they get sassy." She laughed at that and nodded.

"Well I would hate to leave Ruth all alone and bored. What

time do you want me there?"

Victory felt pretty sweet. "Four, but I'll just pick you up and we can all ride together. No need to waste gas." Or to waste my precious Georgia time. Every time I saw her I was only left wanting to spend more and more time with her. I needed to figure out what sort of spell she had me under.

"Alright, I'll see you then." She waved to Ruth and gave me a sweet little smile.

9

Georgia

My eyes were seeing things. After so many days straight of researching and writing on repeat, I could hardly remember my own name. When I wrote for clients I typically finished a piece in a day or two. My articles had never been longer than five thousand words. So, they were finished in eight hours or less depending on how much research they required.

This book felt more like a marathon. There was no relief in sight other than the bagels and lattes left at my door each morning. I allowed myself fifteen minutes to eat and enjoy the food while thinking about the man who delivered it before diving back in.

I definitely needed fresh air and a change of scenery. And to never look at a computer screen again. Maybe this town had a library and I could check out some books instead of reading online. Though they were probably outdated and taking the time to go to the library would cut into my writing time.

As I got ready for Ashton's practice I found myself staring

at my closet for far too long. What is the proper attire for a volleyball practice? Ruth and Ash saw me in nothing short of pajamas this morning so it shouldn't matter. But I was totally overthinking this.

I forced my brain to quiet down and reached for athletic clothes that looked the comfiest. A knock sounded at my door while the hood of my hoodie got stuck over my head. I yanked it down and hurried down the stairs with rushed hands pushing my hair back into a ponytail.

I opened the door and turned to walk back into my kitchen. I started babbling nervously, "Hey! Sorry I lost track of time. I was thinking that maybe I could bring some of the stuff I baked the other day to practice so the kids could take some home after. Would that be okay?"

"I want a treat!" Ruth offered with her hand held out. I glanced at Ashton and waited for approval.

"Just one, are there any cookies left?" He asked cautiously. I gave him a smirk before continuing to box up treats.

"Nope, they were so tasty I ate them all up myself." I shot back. His eyes widened as he looked me up and down to check for serious signs of illness. "Here Ruth, how about a cupcake with sprinkles?"

"Yes, please!" I took one from the plastic container I was setting cupcakes in and placed it in her hand. Ashton's hand mussed up her hair.

"Okay, I'm ready now. Let's go watch some volleyball." Quick hands snatched the containers from me. I unhooked my purse by the entryway and followed them out the door.

The car ride involved a confession from Ruth about how she and her dad were the people who had been ding dong ditching me every day. I put on my best shocked face and turned all the way around in my seat to look at her. Her giggles lasted for the rest of the car ride.

Rosewood's high school was much smaller than what I was used to. Walking around the main school, there was a separate building in the back that served as the school's gym and auditorium. Though it was cozy, it was also well taken care of.

Ashton walked us over to the bleachers and set down his gym bag before bending over to rifle through it. "So, I've got anything you might need in here. Snacks, water, juice." He slid his gaze over to Ruth. "Only one juice for Ruth. The other is for Georgia, got it?"

Ruth's bun bobbed with her head as she nodded. "Got it."

His gaze slid back to me. "And no more baked goods for Ruth either, please. She gets stomach aches when she has too much sugar."

My ponytail bounced this time. "Got it."

"Okay, you two. Let me know if you need anything else. I'll be right over-" He holds his hand to his eye like a telescope. "There. If you need me." He turned back to us with a grin.

That smile could light up entire oceans. Fuck lighthouses.

I watched him jog back down the bleachers and appreciated his cut calves and thighs. His athletic shorts fit him nicely, so my eyes were drawn to his ass next. Every part of his body that I had seen was cut with nothing but lean muscle. It made me want to see the parts that I hadn't gotten to yet.

When I turned to ask Ruth if she wanted a juice now, her stare made me pause. Her eyes and nose were squinted up all tight like she was trying to look closely at my face. She huffed and asked, "Do you have freckles? I can't tell."

"Freckles? Not right now, but I usually get a few in the

62

summer. I haven't been in the sun enough yet." I explained. That made her face scrunch up even more.

"The sun draws on your freckles?" She sounded confused.

"Well sort of, I'm not sure exactly how it works but the sun causes some people to get freckles." I worded carefully. Her eyes widened and I felt like I had just given a very wise piece of information by her reaction.

"I drew freckles on my daddy. They were purple." Now that piece of information was way better than mine.

"Oh yeah? I bet he loved that." Her laugh turned a few heads from the high school boys lining up. A few waved our way.

Volleyballs were rolled out in a cart onto the court and the kids started stretching. Ruth made sure to whisper all of the names she knew and very specific details of things they had done before.

"That one with the red hair is Longbert. But daddy calls him Shortbert because he says he doesn't jump high enough when he blocks. And Johnson is really bad at serving so make sure you cover your head when it's his turn."

After I had the low down on every male high school volleyball player in Rosewood, the real practice began. Ruth let me know each drill they were doing and what was coming up next. Ashton made sure to catch my eye every so often. I wondered if he thought I was uncomfortable, but this was the most fun I had had in a long time.

Usually socializing was more stressful than fun for me. But being able to observe and listen to Ruth talk was great. There was no pressure to perform.

About halfway through practice a teacher near my age walked into the gym. She waved at Ashton and I felt a tiny bit of panic tighten my throat. The curly headed teacher turned to walk our way, waving at Ruth. Suddenly I felt less comfortable.

Her long polka dot dress flowed with her steps as she headed towards us. She had on huge glasses and her curly brown hair was pulled back into a half up casual hair style. As she got closer I realized the earrings she was wearing were little cat faces.

"Hey Ruth! Who's your friend?" She stood at the next step down from where we were sitting. "I'm Reese Finch, it's nice to meet you!"

"Hey, I'm Georgia Mitchell." I smiled and shook her hand.

"She's our new neighbor! We ding dong ditched her house," Ruth added.

Reese laughed a little and sat down. "You'll have to give me pointers on how to ding dong ditch, Ruth. It's been a while." She turned to me now. "I'm a teacher here and I've been friends with Ashton since we were kids so I come to sit with Ruth sometimes."

I nodded. "I've never witnessed a volleyball practice in my life so I'm just here to learn. Ruth has been a great teacher so far."

"She's a smart kid. If only we could get her into books. She would be the new age Einstein." Reese leaned back to pinch Ruth's elbow. Ruth responded with the best slow blink I have ever seen.

"You don't like reading? You know I'm writing a book right?" How could a kid not like books? I was especially shocked because I felt like Ruth was very similar to how I was as a kid.

"Daddy told me. I've never known anybody who wrote a book before." She looked back at the court.

I decided to let the reading thing go. The last thing a kid who didn't like reading needed was some adult forcing them

64

to try. Reese started talking about her class to Ruth so I turned back to the practice going on and tuned out.

After their quick chat Reese stood up and said she needed to finish grading some papers. "I'm glad she has company. I hope we see each other again soon, maybe you could come to weekend practice with us."

Moving to a small town had severely boosted my social status. Two invitations to hang out in one day meant I was a new woman. I eagerly responded, "Of course, that sounds fun."

She seemed genuinely happy at my answer and retreated out of the gym.

As soon as Reese left Ruth continued sharing her volleyball insights with me. During her explanation of dolphin dives she stopped and turned to me. "Daddy said your book was about relationships."

"Yeah, that's right. I'm writing about how to find relationships that are worth it in the long run."

Her head tilted. "Like boyfriend relationships right?" I couldn't help but snort.

"Sort of, any kind of romantic relationship really." I turned in my seat to give her my full attention. I was really hoping this conversation was not going to be any more in depth on that.

"So you have a boyfriend? Or a girlfriend?" She sounded very confused.

"No I don't, but I have had boyfriends in the past." Her eyes squinted now in disapproval.

She tipped her chin up and offered some advice. "You should have one, that would help you write your book. Daddy said it would take a long time, but that's because you don't have a relationship to write about."

This kid was wise beyond her years. I had no argument for that logic. "Not a bad idea Ruth, but I don't have time to get in a relationship. I've got a book to write."

Her face scrunched up again. So I decided to do a quick topic change. "Want a juice?"

Face un-scrunched, she nodded. I offered her the juice box and she insisted I unwrap the straw and stick it in first. Her happy wiggle at the first sip warmed my heart.

Suddenly pain bloomed all over the left side of my face. My neck snapped towards Ruth as the volleyball hit my cheek so hard I felt whiplash. The ball bounced off my face and knocked the juice right out of her small hand. Purple stained her shirt and splashed all over the bleachers and gymnasium floor.

I stared at Ruth. She was frozen in shock. The kind of frozen that kids give you for a few seconds before they decide if they will burst into tears or laugh it off. So I did my best to avoid the first option.

My laugh rang around the quiet gym as everything fell silent. Ruth turned her eyes to me and her mouth slowly turned from a small frown into a smile. "Aw man, that must have been Johnson huh?"

That earned a full belly laugh. I joined in and kept one eye on Ashton. He looked pissed. He called over the kid who I assumed served the ball. An intense conversation later and the kid looked mortified as he walked up to us.

I cut him off before he had the chance. "Hey, it's totally okay. Mistakes happen and my face is perfectly fine." I tried smiling extra big to show him it really wasn't a big deal.

His grimace didn't match my smile. He spoke loudly, "I am so sorry. I promise it will never happen again."

I held up my hands and calmly reasoned, "Don't be. Really, no harm done. Don't worry about it."

He apologized one last time before turning around and getting back in position to continue playing the practice match they were doing. Ashton walked over this time.

"Hey, are you okay? Do we need to get you to a doctor?" He asked with his voice speaking so softly. His hand tilted up my chin to get a better look at me. As if my eyes held all of the answers to his questions. I warmed at his touch and looked down.

"I'm perfectly fine. It just shocked me. Did you know your daughter can see into the future?" I nervously chatted. He did not seem convinced that I was okay. He bent down to gather all of our stuff that was spread out over the bleachers to shove it into his bag.

"Is it over already? They're still playing down there." I pointed as if he wasn't already aware of the match in full swing a few feet away from us.

He slung the bag over his shoulder and offered me a hand. "The assistant coach will stay while they finish this last game. Johnson will be doing an extra lap after. But we should go home. That hit you pretty damn hard."

"You're giving the kid too much of a hard time. It was an accident. And I'm perfectly fine." That poor kid was being punished for my slow reflexes. Way to make a first impression on my new town. I took his hand and stood and he reached for Ruth next.

"He needs to learn to control where the ball goes. Even if you are fine, that could have hit Ruth. Or seriously hurt you." That made my stomach sink a little. He took the steps down the bleachers one at a time with Ruth. "You okay, love bug? I saw the ball knock the juice out of your hand."

Ruth smiled up at him. "Do I get another one now?" He reached into his bag to pull out the second juice and stabbed the straw into the box. Once they were firmly on solid ground he handed it over to her.

With one hand pressed to Ruth's head, Ashton nodded for me to walk ahead of them. We safely exited the gym without catching any more stray balls.

10

Ashton

I was officially the biggest jerk on the planet. After convincing Georgia to leave her house for the first time in days this was the experience she got. A volleyball right to the face. She seemed uncomfortable when all the guys were over helping her move so I wanted to make a good impression this time.

My failure made my entire body tense as I drove us back home from practice. Georgia kept glancing at the way my hands were strangling the steering wheel. At least Ruth was happy. She could not stop chirping about how she predicted Johnson would hit somebody.

Georgia leaned in a little and spoke quietly. "Hey, it really isn't a big deal. The poor car didn't do anything to you."

I choked out a laugh and forced my hands to relax. "I just wanted you to have a good time. My big plans to show off Rosewood weren't all that spectacular."

Her silence prompted me to look over at her. Georgia was usually pretty easy to read but I had no clue what she was thinking this time. "I had a really great time actually. The ball to the face didn't feel great but Ruth was giving me a run down of everyone. She's really fun to talk to. And it was nice to see a volleyball match live for the first time."

She took in a deep breath and continued her analysis. "Ashton, you really don't need to worry about me having a good time. My standards are pretty low. I consider drinking hot chocolate in summer a proper celebration, remember?"

I wasn't sure if that made me feel worse or better. She mentioned the other night that she moved here because she wanted to belong somewhere. I vowed to prove to Georgia Mitchell that Rosewood was worth belonging to.

"Will you let me have a re-do sometime? I promise there will be no physical harm involved." A bright smile returned to her face.

We pulled into the driveway and I parked the truck. The fire in her eyes returned as she replied sassily, "Only if I get to see you play next time. I want to see the Olympian in action."

Now my smile matched hers. Fire lit my own eyes as I challenged, "Maybe if you're lucky, peach."

I hopped out of the car and left her glaring at me through the window. Throwing open the door to the back seat, I went to help Ruth but found her sleeping.

Georgia came to stand beside me and smiled when she saw why I was staring. I turned away from the truck and whispered, "I'll walk you to your door first and then carry her inside."

"You are such a dad. I think I can manage the 20 feet to my front door on my own." She whispered while turning. I followed her anyway. When she reached the door she spun around to face me.

"Persistent aren't you?" She huffed but the way she bit her

lip to hide a smile told me she wasn't too upset. I scoffed and hung my head to stare at our shoes. Knowing her, talking with her, and feeling her look at me was overwhelming.

I looked back up at her anyway. "Just want to make sure you get home safe. Rosewood is a dangerous place after all. You never know when to expect an attack from a rogue volleyball player."

She laughed at my dumb joke and my heart fluttered. Never in my life have I felt this giddy over anything other than volleyball. I had only known her for a week and just a laugh had me wrapped around her finger.

"I really did enjoy going with you guys. And I needed the break, my brain was beginning to turn into mashed potatoes." She twisted a ring on her finger again.

I realized I was staring at her hands when I looked up at her. I confidently insisted, "We'll do it again. But better. You should explore your new town a little more. Ruth and I are happy to be tour guides if you ever need us." Or want us. But I didn't say that part out loud.

Now my eyes got stuck staring at her lips. They were the perfect shade of pink and looked soft and inviting. All of Georgia began to look soft and inviting as I learned more about her. My pretty neighbor reminded me of a prickly pear. Nick made me try one once. It was hard and prickly on the outside but when you peeled back the skin it was soft and sweet on the inside.

My feet took me a step closer to Georgia until I was looming over her. My nose angled down and my hand lifted up to hold her chin. I tilted her jaw up until we were nearly nose to nose. She let out a short breath and waited. My brain short circuited as I leaned in to kiss her cheek before letting go of her jaw.

I quickly turned on my heel, unsure of what the hell just came over me. I called out a quick goodbye and left her standing at her doorstep. My cheeks were flaming by the time I reached my truck and pulled Ruth out of her booster seat.

Ruth took a nap for about an hour while I mentally self-destructed. I was losing my mind over a kiss on the cheek. But maybe that wasn't true at all. It was the way I felt so strongly about her that scared me the most.

After Ruth's mom left us I signed both of us up for therapy. I had Ruth and no time or energy to feel bitter about women leaving me. Ruth was so little she didn't fully understand what happened. She cried every night for three months straight because she wanted her mommy. At the six month mark she stopped asking about her entirely.

Now three years later Ruth and I rarely ever spoke about her mom. Sometimes I saw her watching kids at the park with their mothers, but she never said anything. I had never even considered what would happen if I met someone and fell in love. How would she react? She was so guarded after what happened. How could I risk hurting her like that again?

I was getting way too ahead of myself. Georgia and I were barely friends, much less in love. But I needed to call Ruth's old therapist and ask for her opinion on how to approach the subject if anything did happen.

Ruth's steps on the stairs pulled me out of my spiral. I asked for her help with cooking dinner and she happily agreed. We fell asleep early that night after watching a movie about a lost clown. I related to it a lot.

* * *

A week later I woke to the sound of giggling. I heard soft footsteps going around my bed and a noise I didn't recognize. My eyes remained closed as I soaked in the last few minutes of peace before starting my day.

Warm light blinded me through my eyelids. I winced and sat up to figure out what the hell Ruth was doing. I huffed, "Good morning to you too, sunshine."

She had pulled my black out curtains apart to reveal the morning sun pouring directly into my window. I hoped to God my brother never told her about how we used to wake each other up as kids with freezing cold water. I sleepily asked, "What's with all of this? Am I late for something?"

She smiled and started climbing up to sit on the bed. After situating herself in the bright light with me, she curled up under my arm. Then she explained, "Georgia said the sun can give you freckles."

I must look like some kind of monster for my baby girl to go through such extreme measures to improve my beauty. "Oh, yeah?"

"Mhm, she said she gets freckles in the summer. Because she spends time in the sun." She paused for me to catch up. Which meant this was serious stuff. When I didn't react she explained slowly, as if I was a dimwit. "Georgia needs a boyfriend."

The jump from freckles to boyfriend had my mind reeling. The confusion in my voice was obvious. "A boyfriend? Did she tell you that?"

"She said she had boyfriends in the past. But not anymore. I think she needs one now for her book," Ruth explained. Maybe my baby girl really did have visions of the future. I couldn't agree with her more. But there was no way I could tell her that.

"I'm sure she'll get a boyfriend when she's ready. What does that have to do with you waking me up at 7 a.m. with the scorching sun in my eyes?" I squeezed her closer.

"Georgia gets freckles in the summer. So I was thinking we need some too." At least they weren't made with permanent marker this time.

I obnoxiously yawned and stretched as much as my body would go. Ruth laughed and pushed me off of her. "How about we do that at the beach then? Very sunny there. Suntanning in bed isn't as effective. The sun isn't as strong through a window."

I wasn't sure if that was scientifically correct, but hopefully it meant I wouldn't get any more blinding wake up calls. Ruth sat up eagerly and pleaded, "Can we go today?"

"Not today, but we will go sometime soon. I promise. Maybe the guys can come with us?" She nodded. I scooped her up in my arm and swung the both of us out of bed. She clung to my arm and laughed as I walked us to her room and sat her back down.

"Uncle Nick can make frozen grapes again!" She proudly added. I would never understand the connection my daughter had with my brother. She idolized him for putting grapes in a damn freezer.

"Yeah, yeah, I'm sure he'll make some for you. What do you want to wear today? Shorts or dress?" I asked distractedly.

She leapt off her bed and joined me at her dresser. Thirty minutes later she was in a green dress with her hair in two braids. We made our way downstairs and I started scrambling eggs. Ruth reminded me, like always, to not over-scramble hers. Which was a term my lovely brother taught her.

I set a plate of non-over-scrambled eggs in front of Ruth.

Grabbing an energy drink out of my fridge, I sat down with my own plate and started eating. Our breakfasts were usually the only time the house was silent other than when we were sleeping. We were so focused on filling our stomachs, neither of us had time to talk.

My phone rang with Nick's name popping up. "Speak of the devil," I muttered.

"Who is it?" She said through a mouthful of egg.

"Uncle Nick." I picked the phone up after shoveling eggs into my own mouth. "What do you want? It's not even eight in the morning."

"There's a huge business conference going on at the hotel downtown today. Apparently they were having it catered by some bullshit corporate place, but they bowed out this morning. They want me to provide three hundred people with food for lunch in four hours." Shit.

Nick's restaurant was doing well but this was only his first year of business. He told me big catering events could be the difference between him breaking even and making a profit this year. I helped out when he first opened eight months ago with trivial stuff like serving and making food runs when he was short staffed.

"You know I can't cook. How can I help?" I looked over at Ruth. Finding last minute day care that wasn't Nick was going to be difficult.

"I have about a hundred answers to that. Can you get here? Do you think Reese can watch Ruth?" He must have been really desperate. My brother would usually use every excuse under the sun to see Ruth.

"It's the last week of school, she's working. I'll call Clay and ask." My brother huffed in response.

The background noise coming from my phone already sounded like chaos. He shouted over the noise, "He's here. Is there anyone else?" I had an idea but it was a long shot.

"I'll figure something else out. Be there soon." I hung up and turned to Ruth staring. She was quite the eavesdropper so I didn't feel the need to catch her up.

"How would you feel about maybe spending a few hours with Georgia?" I questioned. Her eyes brightened. I loved the fact that she liked Georgia after only meeting her a few weeks ago. She nodded quickly with her cheeks puffed up like a hamster.

I chewed slowly, figuring out how best to go about this. "Okay, when you're done we can go over and ask Georgia. She might say no so don't get too excited. She has to write her book, remember? So if she does say yes you need to be very respectful and let her write."

I gave her my best stern look and she nodded again. Somehow she shoveled eggs into her mouth even faster now. I was about to tell her to slow down so she didn't choke when I realized she finished her last bite.

"Ready, daddy!" I laughed.

"Okay, can you go grab your shoes? They're on the bench by the door. I still have a few bites left." She hurried off only to ask me two more times where her pink sandals were.

We knocked together on Georgia's door twice. Georgia opened it and I was instantly reminded of what happened the last time I saw her after I dropped her off. My face heated and I instinctively put my hand on the back of my neck.

Today she wore a soft looking sweater and tight leggings that showed off the curves of her legs. Those thighs were made for holding onto. My hands felt the urge to run over those sweet curves and memorize every inch of her.

I needed to focus. I squeezed my eyes shut before rambling, "Good morning. So, it's totally okay to say no but my brother is having a small issue at work that he needs my help with. Is there any way Ruth can stay with you until twelve? She can be quiet as a mouse. And she has an invisibility cloak. You won't even notice she's there."

Georgia tilted her head and laughed. "No need to be quiet or invisible. Of course she can come hang out. We didn't get to finish our lesson about volleyball last time."

I put both of my hands over Ruth's ears like earmuffs. "Seriously, totally okay to say no. He just really needs my help and everyone else we know is either also helping or working. You won't hurt our feelings. I know you're busy."

"Do you ever listen to anything I say?" She smirked and my face heated even more. Would my brain ever get used to Georgia Mitchell?

"Yeah, you said something that sounded like maybe." I snarked back. She rolled her eyes and held out a hand to Ruth.

"I said of course. Now go on, help with your emergency." She shooed me away off of her doorstep. I turned around one last time to triple check with a thumbs up. She returned her own gesture behind Ruth's back.

The biggest dumb ass smile was plastered on my face as I walked to my truck and shoved the keys in the ignition. I checked my phone one last time before putting it away and reversing. Someone knocking on my window made me jump.

"Hey! I just realized I don't have your number. I figured you might want updates on Ruth or it's probably good to have in case of an emergency," Georgia chirped. I couldn't believe I didn't think of that. I really needed to figure out how the hell to focus around her.

I pulled out my phone as she recited her number. Then I texted her so she would have mine too. She backed up still facing me and gave me a little wave. I waved and blew a kiss to Ruth who still stood on the porch. She screamed, "Bye, daddy!"

When I got to Nick's I saw it was closed to the general public. I knocked on the door until Clay noticed me and walked around the counter to let me in. "Hey, man. Glad you could make it."

"I guess we signed up to be on-call sous chefs when Nick bought this place huh?" He huffed out a laugh and nodded.

In the back I was met with four other volleyball players from our league including my brother. I interrupted the chaos, "Hey, where do you want me?"

He looked up for less than a minute before asking, "Where the hell is Ruth?"

"She's staying with Georgia." I answered. His head lifted to stare at me again.

"Georgia? The neighbor." He stated with disbelief in his voice. Oh, he was totally going to make a thing out of this. I didn't want to make a thing out of it. I wasn't even sure what that thing would be.

"Yes, Georgia the neighbor." I mocked reluctantly. Everyone else lifted their heads to shoot looks at each other as well. It was pretty abnormal for Ruth to hang out alone with anyone other than Nick or Reese. I sighed and offered, "It's for a few hours and Ruth really likes her. Not a big deal."

Another pause, Nick put down his knife and grabbed a piece of paper from the table behind him. "Right, here, I need you to run over to the depot and grab all of this." He handed me a scroll of various food items. Okay maybe not a scroll, but a very long list.

"Got it, I'll be back when I'm done." He stopped me with a hand on my shoulder.

"Are you sure you're okay with this? I can have someone else run it if you need to get back to Ruth," He spoke quietly. Not this again. I pushed his hand off.

"Ruth likes her and wanted to go, I made sure before we asked. Georgia has my number and she promised to send updates. I'm good and these scrubs are illiterate so I'm your best bet." A few slices of uncooked bacon and a single cherry tomato was thrown at me.

I walked out of the store and headed to do the most high-stakes grocery trip of my life.

11

Georgia

This morning I was surprised to find Ashton and Ruth at my doorstep again. After watching him rush off last week I figured he regretted kissing my cheek. That was the first time I had seen Ashton's confidence waver and I spent the rest of the night thinking about it afterwards.

When he left Ruth with me I decided there was no way I was going to write while she was here. I was unpracticed with kids but not an asshole. So we made our way to the kitchen to brainstorm some ideas of what to do while Ashton was gone. I decided that leaving my house wasn't an option because I wasn't sure if Ashton would be okay with that and I also didn't have a booster seat in my car.

I was really missing out on the latte that they brought me every day. My body quickly got accustomed to the extra caffeine boost. Instead of caving, I pulled out my kettle and prepared a tea bag. Turns out little girls don't like hot tea so I only made the one for myself.

A lightbulb went off as I took the first sip. "Ruth, do you like baking?"

"I help daddy cook sometimes. Uncle Nick says I'm good at it." She offered helpfully from her seat at the stool.

I bent down to rifle through my cabinet filled with cookbooks. Showing Ruth the wonderful world of books probably wasn't my job. But I could at least be a good influence and gently guide her into books. Hopefully this would be the least intimidating way possible.

I found what I was looking for and stood back up. Walking around the counter to where Ruth sat, I stretched and sat down on the stool next to her. The big cookbook in my hands was the most colorful one I had. I set it down in between us and flipped it open.

"This one has a bunch of silly recipes. We can make pretty much anything in this book. Do you want to flip through it and pick out something?" I subtly nudged it closer to her.

I had no idea where this aversion came from so the second she told me she wasn't interested I would drop it. She glanced down and took in the bright and colorful page. Her little hand reached out to flip to the first actual recipe.

Trying not to seem too eager, I added, "I have a lot of different sprinkles and stuff too so we can even decorate most of them the way the book does."

She flipped to another page. Her little face was very concentrated at taking in all of the pictures. I couldn't help but take a quick picture while she was looking through.

Several minutes later she continued flipping silently. As she continued through the book she decided more quickly which interested her and which weren't worth her time. Ultimately she landed on a page with 'Sprinkle Explosion Cupcakes'.

"I like this one. Can we make it?" She asked with wide eyes.

She looked up from the book for the first time in ten minutes. I took that alone as a win.

I skimmed the recipe and was happy to find it was pretty basic. The only trick was that you had to cut a hole after they were done baking to funnel sprinkles inside of the actual cupcake. I happily chimed, "We can! Do you want me to read to you what it says?"

She nodded excitedly and I began reading. After the description was over she squeaked. "Sprinkles inside? How will we see them?"

I let out an airy laugh. I turned the page to the next spread which had more pictures. One showed the cupcake cut in half with sprinkles pouring out of the middle and onto the table the cupcake was set on. She gasped.

"I have never had a cupcake like this before! Only with sprinkles on top!" She was amazed and emphasized the on top part. Her hands formed movements to further show how cupcakes are normally sprinkled.

I laughed. "This will be my first time too. It will be a new baking adventure for the both of us. Sounds pretty cool though, we're going to need a lot of sprinkles."

I got up to wash my hands. Then I turned to Ruth and realized she was too small to reach the sink. How did kids wash their own hands? Did I need to lift her? I looked around at my limited options.

Ruth figured it out for me. "Do you have any steps? Daddy has a step for me to stand on."

"Oh yes, like a step ladder? Let me go grab it. It's in the closet." I brought it back and she looked at it a little funny. I pushed it up against the sink and held her elbow as she took the steps up to wash her hands.

82

"This is bigger than the one daddy has. But I like that because I get to be taller." I laughed again and made sure she got down safely. Moving the ladder over to the island this time, I decided it would be easiest to set everything up over there so she wouldn't have to keep getting up and down.

"Alright, next we need to get all of our ingredients and measure them." I slid the cookbook over to Ruth's new position at the island. I leaned over her shoulder and slid my pointer finger underneath the words I was reading. "So here it says ingredients. And lists them off down here. Can you read the number and I'll read the words?"

She nodded and straightened her posture. "I know my numbers. Daddy and I practice with flashcards. He forgets them sometimes."

"I do too so I'm glad to have you here. So what's this first number?"

"Three," She read and held up the number with her fingers too.

"Okay, so three cups of flour. Let me grab the flour." I paused. "Wait, I forgot the most important step! We need aprons so we don't get our clothes all messy."

After tying my own apron, I folded the waist of an apron up for Ruth and tied it tightly around her waist so it didn't fall down too much. I placed flour down on the counter and grabbed all of the measuring cups and spoons we would need. A big bowl was placed in front of Ruth and I showed her how to scoop up the flour and count to three while we put them in the bowl.

We continued the process for seven more ingredients. I stopped to snap a picture of Ruth while she was measuring the last teaspoon of salt. If I had a kid I would appreciate as many updates as possible, so I sent it over to Ashton before we moved onto mixing.

Ruth and I made a good team as we mixed, poured, and popped all of the cupcakes into the oven. Moving onto icing was when it started to get messy. I forgot to warn Ruth about powdered sugar when she dumped an entire cup and a huge cloud poofed back up in our faces. She hesitated and I laughed.

"Powdered sugar always does that. It's very messy which is why we have our aprons." I grabbed a pinch out of the bag and flicked it into the air. The delight in her eyes made me realize that might not be the best thing to teach a kid.

"You can try to throw a pinch too if you want. But only one, we need the sugar to go in the icing," I offered.

Her hand dove into the bag and she got out a handful of it. She threw the sugar straight up in the air and it landed in a light dusting all over her hair and the island. I tried my best to stifle a laugh.

"It's like snow!" Her tiny voice squealed. She eyed the bag again.

"Yes, very messy snow. Alright we need one more cup, let's measure it and put it in." She did so and I quickly rolled up the bag of powdered sugar and put it away.

After our ingredients were ready for the icing I moved in with a hand mixer. Typically I would start mixing icing on the lowest setting, but I liked seeing Ruth laugh so I started on the highest.

Powder sugar exploded up in our faces and nearly got as far as the ceiling. I drastically underestimated how much would fly out. Ruth burst out laughing, bending over her ladder. I laughed too while taking in how much of a mess my kitchen was. That was a problem for future-me to deal with.

11

I retrieved the powdered sugar bag and added a bit more to account for the loss of sugar in my accident. Then I started mixing on the lowest setting until we had soft fluffy icing. I dipped my pinky in and tasted it. Thankfully no icing was harmed in the process. Ruth tasted too and agreed.

We proceeded to color the icing and I showed Ruth how to put it in piping bags. The cupcakes had just come out of the oven when Ashton called. I took off my oven mitts and answered it on speaker so Ruth could say hi.

"Hey, how is helping your brother going?" I asked.

He huffed. "Fan freaking tastic. I'm a glorified errand boy." Ruth giggled. "Is everything going okay? I got your picture, what are you guys making?"

Ruth answered for me. "Daddy, it's a surprise. The coolest surprise ever. Georgia is teaching me how to bake. And we made a mess."

"I promise I will clean up any mess that is made." Ashton added quickly.

"I can assure you, most of it was made by me. And there might be a little bit on Ruth." I looked over her hair and the tops of her shoulders that were speckled with white.

He laughed at that. "So everything is good? I've got a couple hours left and then I'll be done."

"Everything is great. Do you want to talk to Ruth for a minute? I have to use the bathroom anyway," I offered. He agreed and I made sure to help Ruth down from the ladder before going upstairs to use my bathroom.

I returned to Ruth describing an explosion. Maybe that wasn't the best way to start off my babysitting career. Ashton seemed happy though as he laughed and added sounds so she would know he was listening.

85

When she saw me, she quickly ended the conversation and handed the phone over. "Oh, daddy Georgia is back. We need to get back to baking. Bye."

Ashton spoke before I could hang up, "I really appreciate you doing this. I owe you free moving service for the rest of your life."

"Not at all, we're having the time of our lives. I never knew I needed a baking partner before, but I might steal her from you from now on." I heard a car door slam on his end.

He sighed and sounded dreamy, "I'm sure we can have something arranged, peach. I've gotta get back to my errands. Thank you so much again. I'll be there in a couple of hours."

I felt the still too hot cupcakes with the back of my hand. "Okay, sounds good. We'll see you when you get here. Bye, Ashton."

"Bye, peach." He hung up and I took a second to breathe. Was I really starting to like a silly pet name?

I turned to Ruth who was petting Tweet. "We have to wait for the cupcakes to cool off. Do you want to watch TV or something in the meantime?"

I looked down at our clothes. We really were messy. My sweater would never recover from the powdered sugar and flour caked into it. I needed to put towels down over the couch before we went anywhere near it. Ruth cheered, "Yes! We can watch Bluey."

After approximately two Bluey episodes we were ready to start icing. I was showing Ruth my extensive sprinkle selection when a furry friend hopped onto the counter to join us.

I shrieked "Tweet, get down you lunatic!"

She quickly hopped down from the counter but her paw prints already had some of the powdered sugar residue.

86

Small white powdered paw prints now trailed throughout my kitchen. Ruth slapped a hand over her mouth to hide her giggle.

A knock on the door surprised me. I checked the clock again. We were supposed to have thirty more minutes before Ashton came back. I told Ruth to stay still and I went to open the door.

I was greeted with a face almost as messy as mine. His hair was hidden with a backwards baseball cap but it had marks of what looked like flour on it. His shirt was covered in more residue of what I assumed was food.

"Hey, he let me off early. Apparently I'm no good with a fryer." I paused in my staring to back up and let Ashton into my house.

"Your brother owns a restaurant?" I asked dumbly. How did I not know this?

"Yeah, today he had a huge catering order come in at the last minute. So he needed all hands on deck. This is his first year so I've been helping out where I can." I nodded and led him to Ruth.

I paused by the door to let him take in my messy kitchen. I glanced down to see there were marks of flour covering his ass too. His jeans were wrecked.

Then he froze in the doorway of my kitchen. I laughed and Ruth frowned at her dad. She grumpily complained, "We weren't done yet! I was deciding what sprinkles to funnel." Her arms crossed.

Ashton quickly walked up to her with a mischievous smile and lifted her off the ladder to spin her around. He sarcastically responded, "Nice to see you too, honey bee. Glad you missed me."

Ruth giggled and he set her back down. I interrupted their

roughhousing, "It's actually good that you're here. This next part is new for me too and we might need extra hands."

I smiled at him and then paused. "Oh, unless you guys have other things to do today?"

He shook his head and looked down at the island where the powder sugar mess and unfrosted cupcakes sat. "No place we'd rather be." He smiled up at me and ruffled Ruth's hair.

One sentence and I was already flustered. Damn him and his stupid angel face and messy clothes. Did I mention he looked hot as hell in a backwards hat?

I turned around so I wouldn't get distracted by his smile and grabbed the frilliest apron I own. I offered it to him and he put it on without hesitation. The contrast between his huge six foot four frame and muscles covered partially by a tiny strawberry patterned apron with ruffles was hilarious. He cracked his knuckles and stood across from me next to Ruth. "So what's next?"

The three of us concentrated deeply on cutting out small holes in the cupcakes and using a funnel to fill them with sprinkles. We chatted while we worked and decided on adding different sprinkles to each cupcake.

"Okay, now we just need to frost and decorate." I looked up at Ashton. "Do you know how to use a piping bag?"

He smirked. "Yeah, I can pipe pretty well." Did he just- . He held eye contact. He totally meant that kind of pipe.

I handed him the bag with blue icing. His hand purposefully grazed mine as I pulled away. "Have at it then." I said hastily. I turned the cookbook to him while my face felt like it was on fire. "We want it to look like the picture. So you have to pipe it in a swirl."

He continued to stare at my face. It was probably bright red at this point. "Got it," he replied slowly.

I handed the smaller purple icing bag to Ruth and tried to help her practice on a sheet of paper first. She graduated to her own cupcake and I started on mine.

I felt Ashton's eyes staring at me as I focused on icing cupcakes. He might enjoy teasing but I was not capable of controlling my reactions. I just hoped Ruth didn't pick up on how flustered I was.

"Daddy, we're going to watch a movie later. Are you going to stay?" I was glad Ruth felt comfortable staying with me. Even to the point of staying more than she had to.

Ashton shot me a surprised look. "A movie? What are you watching?"

"I mentioned Charlie and the Chocolate Factory earlier when she was looking at the truffles in the book." I tipped my head towards the cookbook. "I said we could watch it if we had time, but we ended up watching Bluey instead. If you don't mind staying we can all watch it together after."

I really needed a full day of break from writing. I realized yesterday how much I had burned myself out from working for days straight. After today I would get right back on track with a fresh and well rested mind.

"You're sure that's okay? Are you taking a break from writing today?" Ashton worried.

I nodded with a smile. "I need a break. Plus, I always have time for Willy Wonka."

He smiled and quietly muttered. "Lucky guy."

Now he was just trying to fluster me on purpose. My hand reached into the powdered sugar that I left out on the counter and threw a handful across the counter at him. Time froze and my eyes widened at my own actions.

His smile turned downright dirty and he yanked the bag toward his side of the island to grab his own handful. I begged, "Wait, Ashton. We're even. There's no need for retaliation."

He smirked and I lifted my hands to shield my face. White powder flew into my vision seconds later. I looked down and my jaw dropped. Powdered sugar landed all over my apron and sweater and I turned to see it also covered the counter and sink behind me.

Ruth shrieked and made grabby hands at the bag. Ashton handed it over and she grabbed her own handful to throw at her dad. His jaw dropped at the betrayal.

I was the first to laugh and Ruth followed soon after. Ashton lifted Ruth over his shoulder and carried her outside while upside down. Her breathless gulps of air didn't stop until she was set down on the grass. Ashton turned back to me, a smile still on his face.

"I'm going to have to hose the two of you off."

I looked him up and down with a glare. "Speak for yourself, you're no better than us."

He lifted his black t-shirt over his head and it took everything in me not to gasp. He had tattoos covering his shoulder and even a few trailing down his abdomen. His cut muscles were definitely one of a pro athlete. I watched his every move as he took his shirt and beat it against the fence to knock the sugar off.

I was practically drooling at the sight of his back and arm muscles working together to slam the shirt against the fence. It was a scene straight out of one of my late night fantasies that I used to get myself off when my brain wouldn't stop thinking about Ashton at night. I wanted to get down on my knees to lick up his abs with my tongue.

90

He watched me as he put the shirt back on. Taking in his handiwork, he shrugged. A knowing look was sent my way after he caught me staring. I continued to stare at his shirt. Now that I knew what was underneath, I felt a little offended at the fabric.

He broke our gaze and leaned down to brush off Ruth's hair and the mess that had gotten on her dress. I started untying my own apron to dust off as much sugar as I could from my sweater. Once Ashton deemed us clean enough we headed back inside.

"I really will clean this up. Are we done?" Ashton winced at the messy kitchen.

"We still need to add the sprinkles on top, silly goose." Ruth reminded him.

Gathered around the island, we all made the final push to decorate the cupcakes with a multitude of different kinds of sprinkles. We shared high fives after we were done and Ruth insisted on taking the first bite.

She seemed disappointed that her tiny bite wasn't overflowing with sprinkles. "Here, let me try." Ashton stole her cupcake and fit nearly half of it in his mouth before chomping down. As he pulled away sprinkles spilled out into his free hand and on the floor.

Ruth cheered, "Surprise!"

Ashton tried to prevent any further mess but the sprinkles continued to fall until every last one had spilled out of the cupcake. I laughed. My kitchen would never recover, but this was totally worth it.

"Let's go watch Charlie and the Chocolate Factory now please." Ruth scooted down the ladder on her own and headed to the living room.

"So is it any better than the cookies?" I asked.

"I honestly can't taste anything through the sprinkles." His tongue was rainbow-colored as he spoke. I snickered again and offered him a napkin.

He grabbed my outstretched wrist and pulled me closer. His hand raised to my jaw and his thumb rubbed off left over powdered sugar on my cheekbone. His tongue darted out to lick the sugar off of his thumb before grabbing the napkin and wiping off his hands and mouth.

I watched his hand with intrigue before he dropped it back to his side. I had to pull my gaze away before I could form words again. My words were slow, "I think we might have put in a bit too many sprinkles. Do you want anything to drink?"

He nodded. "Yes, water please." I gave him a glass of it. "So, movie time?"

I put away any rogue ingredients and set the dirty bowls and utensils in the sink. I replied tiredly, "Movie time. Are you hungry? Maybe we should order lunch." My stomach was growling as I realized I didn't have breakfast.

"I'll have something delivered. What are you in the mood for?" He asked and grabbed a kitchen towel to dampen it at the sink before wiping down the island.

"Mexican? I want something cheesy." He finished up the island before moving to the counters and the sink. I walked to the closet to grab my broom and dustpan. Having someone who was a stranger to me a few weeks ago help me clean felt odd. Not bad odd, it was nice. I had a strangely comfortable feeling whenever Ashton was around.

After my kitchen was acceptably clean we joined Ruth on the towel-covered couch. Ruth sat on the very end so Ashton sat in the middle of us while I sat on the opposite end. He pulled out his phone and started ordering a delivery service. Tugging on one of Ruth's braids he leaned over to ask if nachos sounded good.

I pulled up the movie and hit play once everyone was settled and all the lights were out. I offered Ruth and Ashton a blanket and grabbed my own. It was frowned upon in my household to watch a movie without a blanket to snuggle up with.

About halfway in I looked over to see Ruth had fallen asleep. My own eyelids were feeling pretty heavy. Baking with a five year old required a lot of mental concentration. I also missed out on my latte this morning so I was minutes away from sleep.

Until I felt a pinky touch mine. My head jerked down to look and I saw Ashton's hand placed right next to mine. I looked at his face and he tilted his head as if he was gauging my reaction. My heart was racing again. He didn't even have to do anything. Ashton's existence alone was enough to make me feel excited.

I lifted my pinky to rest over his. He waited a few seconds before enveloping my hand completely in his. I forced my head to continue staring at the TV as I felt my cheeks flush. He intertwined our fingers and I shuffled over closer so that my feet were now touching his thigh as my legs folded under me.

Casual affection was one of the few things I had severely missed after not being in relationships for a while. Focusing on my career had many benefits, but sometimes I craved being with someone like this. We continued staying silent as my eyelids grew heavy again.

My head rested against his shoulder and I gave in to his comfortable heat. I dozed off and woke up when the doorbell rang. He slowly removed his hand from mine. I sat up and blinked.

"It's just the food, be right back." He whispered. Food. I was so comfortable in sleep I had forgotten how hungry I was.

I stood up and left a still sleeping Ruth alone on the couch. I found Ashton in the kitchen setting down take out boxes. "Good morning, sleepy head." His voice sounded so soft. Like it was calling me home to lay down and fall asleep again.

"Morning, I'm hungry," I grumbled. He chuckled and found the box that belonged to me. I lifted myself onto a stool and ripped open the box to start eating my tacos.

"Did you not eat breakfast?" He asked, still speaking in his sweetly soft voice. I shook my head. These were either the best tacos I had ever had or I was just desperately hungry. Either one was a valid option.

Ashton frowned as his eyebrow furrowed. "Sorry, I forgot to bring you something."

I lifted my eyebrows at him. "You're not responsible for my breakfast. I have plenty of food. I just got distracted by cupcakes."

He sat down next to me with his stool pushed close to mine and opened his own container of food. His thighs were spread wide until his knee rested against mine. We ate in silence. He must have skipped breakfast too. He ate even faster than I did.

By the time we finished eating, the movie was over. We stood over a sleeping Ruth and waited for one of us to break the silence. He spoke first, "Can we do this again sometime?"

His question surprised me. "Yeah, I would like that. I think Ruth had a lot of fun. She even read the cookbook a little for me."

His tired smile was enough to light up my world. "Good. I should take her home to sleep in her bed. Her neck looks like it's about to break." Her head was bent over the couch arm

94

awkwardly.

"Right. Well thanks for bringing her over. And for helping me clean up," I yawned as I finished the sentence. He leaned down to pick up Ruth.

"Anytime, peach. Will you be writing for the next few days?" He spoke softly to not wake up Ruth.

I nodded. "You know it."

I followed him to the front door and opened it for him. "Bye. I'll see you."

He paused as if contemplating saying something else. He spoke slowly, "Bye. Let me know if you need anything okay?"

He really was such a dad. "Of course. You too."

He turned and I watched to make sure they got in their house okay. And yet again I was left wondering about Ashton long after he left.

12

Georgia

The next few days were dedicated to writing again. Although this time I made sure to take breaks and even brought my laptop outside to get some sun. I was doing everything to avoid burnout while also keeping my productivity high.

I was still ahead of schedule after taking the day off with Ruth and Ashton. They returned to their usual routine of ding dong ditch either for breakfast or dinner. I looked at the clock and it was nine a.m. Which probably meant I would be getting dinner today.

A week of writing was when I felt burnt out last time. So I needed to switch it up today. I pulled out my phone and looked up restaurants in Rosewood. I hadn't gone anywhere other than the grocery store since moving into my house. The internet told me there was a diner right down the street so I got dressed and headed out.

A bell chimed as I walked into Reid's Diner. It was a classic looking small town diner with a cozy feel. An older woman sat me at a table near the window and left me with a menu. I quickly found the pancake section and decided on blueberry.

The nice woman returned to take my order and left me with some coffee. I savored the warm cup and took out my laptop. I treated myself with a new environment so why not get some writing done as I wait? No harm in that.

I pushed my laptop to the side when my blueberry pancakes came. I was in the middle of a paragraph so I continued writing. And next thing I knew I had finished the chapter I was working on. Coming up for air, I closed my laptop and dug into my now slightly warm blueberry pancakes.

A couple bites in, I felt like I was being watched. I quickly glanced up and caught the older woman and a male server that looked younger than me turning their heads as I looked up. They were definitely staring. I wasn't wearing anything abnormal, just a tank top and jean shorts. I knew small towns could be conservative but my shorts weren't too short by any means. Did I have something on my face?

My worrying was interrupted by my sister calling. I hadn't talked to her in a while so I answered. The diner was pretty busy with breakfast rush so it was easy to keep my voice down.

"Hey Ardie, what's up?" I asked casually before adding more maple syrup to my pancakes.

"Just checking on you. You haven't called in over a week. How is life in Rosedale?" Oh shit. I just realized I hadn't told her about my book.

"It's great! I actually have good news," I started.

"Oh yeah? Hit me with it." I missed the sound of her voice. Arden was always the sun to my moon. She reminded me to be optimistic and appreciate the small stuff.

I chewed and swallowed before answering. "I got an offer

to ghostwrite a book."

Arden screamed. An actual, very high pitch scream that made me pull my phone away from my ear. "A book offer? How are you not shouting this from the rooftops? You have been dreaming of writing a book since you were like seven."

"I think I did scream a little when I first read the email. But ever since I've pretty much been writing or researching nonstop." I stabbed another bite of pancake.

"Pretty much? What else have you been doing? Please tell me you've made friends. Or met a hot guy. You could really use someone that will show you how to have fun." I sighed.

After the cheek kiss and hand holding with Ashton, I thought a lot about how to tell Arden about him. We clearly weren't dating or anything but it felt wrong to not tell my sister. I was also dying to be able to talk to someone about him.

"Well I have been spending some time with my neighbor. He's a dad and has a five year old daughter."

Arden dramatically sighed. Then the whining began. "Can't you hang out with someone your age? You've always acted so much older than you are." She wasn't wrong. I never enjoyed partying much.

"He's only two years older than me!" I exclaimed defensively. Glancing to my right, I caught the same male server staring at me again.

"Oh, well you should have started with that. Is he hot?"

Of course that was the first question she asked. "He's a retired pro volleyball player. Of course he's hot."

She laughed. "I retract my former statement. You should have started with *that*. Tell me more. I want to know everything."

I took a deep breath. "Well he ended up helping me move

98

my stuff in. He saw I was doing it alone and called up some of his volleyball friends in town to come help. And then his daughter wandered into my house so we met again."

I came up for air before continuing my confession. "I told him about the book offer and he started bringing me lattes and breakfast sometimes. A few days ago he had a family emergency so I babysat his daughter and we baked some cupcakes. They stayed after for a bit while we watched a movie. Oh and they invited me to his volleyball-"

"Woah woah woah. All of this happened and you didn't tell me? He brings you food? You told him about your book before me? What the hell Georgia?" She sounded pissed and impressed at the same time.

"Well his daughter happened to walk in right after I got the book offer so it came up. And then I've been so busy writing I forgot to call you. I'm sorry."

"Don't be sorry. I've been dying for you to find someone. He must make you really happy to take time away from writing," She teased. I frowned a little at that. I think I gave her the wrong idea.

I stabbed, chewed, and swallowed another bite before answering. "We aren't, like, together Arden. Just friends. He's great though. And his daughter is hilarious."

She hummed, clearly not convinced. "Well I'm glad you're making friends then."

The older woman walked past my table for the third time in the last five minutes. I must be doing something wrong. "Hey Arden, I'm at a diner. Can I call you back later?"

"Of course, I'm going to need more details of your hot neighbor when you do. And preferably pictures." I scoffed and hung up on her.

I was actively looking around now, offended at the fact that people kept staring at me. The bell chimed again and I abandoned my search to see who entered. It was Reese, the teacher from Ashton's gym practice.

She walked up to the counter and a very familiar face came out from the kitchen to greet her. He caught my eye while they were talking and Reese turned to look at me too.

She smiled and turned away from Ashton's twin brother. I'm pretty sure his name was Nick but I wasn't the best with names. Reese approached my table and asked to sit down.

I pulled my laptop closer toward my side of the table and gestured for her to sit. "Of course, it's nice to see you again." I said with a smile.

"Yeah, you too. The blueberry pancakes are my favorite. Nick is an amazing cook, and I swear he puts crack in this syrup." She smiled and pointed at the bottle.

I returned the smile. "Definitely, I had no idea he owned this place until just now honestly." Maybe that explained all of the stares then.

Her eyebrows rose. "Really? What a coincidence then. I'm glad I caught you. Can I have your number? Honestly, between volleyball and school I am constantly surrounded by men and have been dying to have a girl friend for once."

I was shocked at her proposal. Was it really this easy to make friends? Either my social skills had significantly improved magically since moving here or Rosewood was a friendly place. Or Ashton had something to do with this.

"That sounds great. Here, text yourself on my phone." I slid it over to her. "My sister has been my only girl friend since college ended. I'm stoked to have someone too."

She smiled and proceeded to message herself. "We should

do something later this week. To kick off the friendship right! Ashton told me you just moved in, is there anything you wanted to do but haven't done yet?"

That list was quite long since I had barely left my house. But there was something that had been bugging me. "This might be boring, but I really want to go plant shopping. I couldn't bring mine with me when I moved and now my house feels so empty without them."

"No way! That sounds so fun, the next town over has a cute little local plant store. I can drive us there and maybe we could grab lunch too." She paused to look down at her phone. "They have a great Thai place."

There was no way making friends was actually this easy. I questioned her again. "Are you sure that sounds fun? We can do something else that you like."

She waved me off. "It's the cutest place. You'll love it and I will be buying another plant to kill by the time the week is through. Is Friday okay?"

Today was Tuesday so that gave me three days to get ahead on work and make up for the time I would lose. "Friday sounds perfect," I chirped.

The bell rang again and I instinctively looked up. Ashton smiled back at me and Ruth waved as if I was some kind of celebrity. I waved back and they walked up to the counter.

A few minutes later Ruth pulled Ashton our way as I was offering to give Reese plant advice. "Georgia, you're at Uncle Nick's! He said he would make me some strawberry french toast with roses. I'll share one with you if you want."

This girl never needed to drink coffee when she grew up if she kept up this energy. I slowed down the pace of the conversation. "That sounds delicious. I had some blueberry pancakes though."

I pointed to my plate and picked up my laptop to put it away in my bag. Ashton leaned in. "Is it okay if we sit with you guys?"

Reese looked at me. I happily replied, "Of course. The more the merrier."

Reese got up and sat next to me so that Ashton and Ruth could sit together. He took the seat against the wall across from me and gave me another smile. Is this what butterflies felt like?

"Sorry to interrupt your writing." He said as I put my bag and laptop away.

"Don't be. I came here to take a break anyway and couldn't resist. If anything you're doing me a favor." I smiled tiredly. Then I turned to Ruth.

"I just found out that Nick owns this place. Do you know why it's called Reid's then?" She laughed at my seemingly silly question.

Ruth pointed at herself as if it was obvious. "That's our name!"

I looked at Ashton for clarification and tilted my head. His playful smile nearly stopped my heart. "Reid is our last name."

"Ashton and Ruth Reid?" My voice raised in pitch. I looked between the two trying to decide if the last name fit them. "How did I not know that?"

He laughed and quipped, "No clue, Georgia Mitchell. Keep up."

How the hell did he know my government name? I didn't remember telling him. I kept my focused stare on him as if he would spill all of his secrets if I only looked at him long enough.

Ruth started telling Reese all about our baking fiasco. Ashton kept his eyes on mine and I felt his foot nudge mine under the table. Goosebumps rose on my arms at the subtle contact. When would this man learn that I couldn't control my reactions around him? I nudged him back and leaned back in my seat.

"And then daddy took a huge bite of the sprinkle surprise cupcake and they spilled everywhere! All over his hands and the floor." Reese laughed and looked between Ashton and me.

"Sounds like you all had a great time. And made some yummy cupcakes." Her smile was teasing as she stared at Ashton and bit into her muffin.

Nick approached the table with three plates. One for Ash, Ruth, and I assumed one for himself. He grabbed a spare chair and pulled it up to the end of the table. "Is it alright if I join?"

He was looking directly at me. I was in no position to deny a man a seat in his own restaurant so I nodded. Ashton reintroduced us and I complimented Nick on his pancakes.

"Thanks, those blueberry pancakes took me a couple of years to perfect the recipe." My eyebrows rose and I nodded.

"He makes good eggs too. He doesn't over scramble them like daddy." Ruth happily added.

I looked back to Ashton and he was rolling his eyes. I bit my lip to hold in a laugh as we held eye contact.

"I heard you watched Ruth so Ash could help me out at the restaurant. Thank you, he really saved my ass," Nick said.

Before I could respond Ruth dove into her second retelling of our day together. Ashton and I turned to each other again and I couldn't help but let a goofy smile take over my face.

If this was what life in Rosewood could be like I could die a happy woman.

13

Ashton

"Daddy! None of my clothes fit." I made my way upstairs to see what Ruth had been huffing and puffing over for the last twenty minutes.

The floor of her room was covered in clothes with her dresser drawers hanging open like the place had been robbed. Ruth sat in the middle of the mess with shorts pulled over her knees but not pulled up all the way.

"They're all too small? I guess you have grown a lot since last summer." I pretended to squish her with my fingers held up in front of my eye.

She just huffed and tears welled up in her eyes. I spoke quickly, "Woah woah, no need to cry over clothes, butter bean. We'll just go get you some better ones. How does that sound?"

She sniffled and rubbed her eyes. I went to her closet to find a dress that would fit. "Here, this should fit. Why don't we go to the mall today? We can invite Uncle Nick. And I think Ryan is in town too."

Her arms lifted and the dress slid down to rest over her

shoulders. A perfect fit. She nodded and I thanked my lucky stars my brother currently owed me a huge favor.

We cleaned her room and she sat down on her bed so I could braid her hair. "I want just one braid today."

"Got it, butter cup. I'll call Nick so we can convince him while I'm braiding." I dialed his number and set my phone on the bed next to us.

"What's up?" Nick sounded dead tired. I made a mental note to buy him a coffee later.

"None of my clothes fit!" Ruth cried out dramatically. "We need you to go shopping with us. That way daddy won't buy me any ugly clothes."

How I was deemed unfit to pick out my own daughter's clothes I would never know. But apparently having the title of uncle in front of your name made you all-knowing. Nick laughed at the insult and I tugged Ruth's hair a little harder than necessary.

"Today?" I saw Ruth's smile in the mirror. She knew she had the fish on the hook, all she had to do was reel him in.

"Yes, do you think Ryan could come too? He always has cool shoes and I want to find some too," She added.

"I'll get him to come. Give us an hour and we'll meet at yours. Do you need breakfast?"

I interjected myself into my daughter and brother's cute little love fest. "No thanks, we already ate. Thanks for coming. I'll drive us there." And with that I hung up.

Ruth sat up much more happily. "Daddy. Do you think there will be rings at the mall?"

"Rings? What kind?" I finished up her braid and tied the end.

"Gold rings. Like the ones Georgia has." Now that I wasn't

expecting.

"I'm not sure, but we can look for some. We need to focus on getting clothes though, right? Gold rings can be our side mission." I wasn't sure whether I should ask why exactly my daughter wanted gold rings like Georgia's. But I decided to leave it at that for now.

Exactly one hour later Nick's car pulled into our driveway. We opened the door to see Nick, Ryan and Will. I pointed at Will. "Since when does he participate in non-work related events?"

Ruth and I walked through the doorway and the guys followed us to my truck. "He doesn't. Which is why I insisted he should come. That CEO bullshit is blackening his soul." Ryan answered.

He paused and looked down at Ruth. "Sorry, I meant bull." She giggled and made eye contact with me. I helped her in the car first. Will sat up front with me as Nick and Ryan slid in the back next to Ruth.

"Well it's nice of you to join. I hope they told you we're going clothes shopping." The deadpan look on his face told me they absolutely did not tell him what we were doing today.

The rest of the car ride was filled with Ruth's questions to Ryan and Nick about various shoes and clothes. I wondered if she noticed the fact that Nick hadn't worn anything other than a black t-shirt and jeans in practically her entire life. We pulled up to the mall and I made Ruth promise to hold my hand and remain within eyesight at all times before getting out of the car.

Ruth looked at each and every item of clothing in every color of the store one by one before deciding if it was worthy of throwing into the cart I pushed. She was currently at the opposite end of an aisle to me staring at polka dot dresses.

Nick looked over at me and started with his favorite question lately. "So, what's going on with you and your neighbor?"

Leave it to my brother to ruin a moment of peace. Ryan and Will perked up at the distraction from talking about if frills were cool or not. I sighed, "We're friends. Ruth really likes her."

That seemed to be my go to line nowadays. The truth was I didn't know what we were and I sure as hell wasn't going to let my brother try to figure it out. Nick continued staring at me.

"This is the same neighbor as before right? What's her name again?" Will asked.

"Georgia." Nick answered for me. "He let her babysit Ruth the other day. And they came into my store yesterday morning. We all sat and ate breakfast together while they made heart eyes at each other."

Ryan seemed very amused at that statement. "Woah, you're dating again? I thought you were done for good at this point. What's it been? Three years?"

"We're not dating and there were no heart eyes." I defended myself.

My brother only shook his head. He snarkily corrected me, "There were definitely heart eyes. I wouldn't be surprised if you were playing footsie under the table."

I forced my face to remain even. There was no way I was admitting that in a million lifetimes. Ryan snickered and Will smiled at the stare down between us.

"You really do like her." Will said.

"Once again, we're friends. Are any of you airheads paying attention here?" I muttered the words with frustration. I

turned to pick up a pair of overalls and pretended to be
interested in them.

Ryan lifted his hand and gestured to me by waving his finger
up and down. "You're doing that thing you always do when
you're lying. You get too defensive, man."

I scowled. "I'm not lying. We are friends."

Nick cut in again. "Maybe so, but you are definitely into her
as more than a friend."

"She's my neighbor. And Ruth's friend. I haven't dated
anyone in three years as Summers so kindly pointed out.
Nothing's happening there," I repeated robotically.

Yet. Nothing was happening there yet. I set down the
overalls.

Will piped up. "But you're considering it. If you're actually
interested you should go for it. After three years of not being
tempted once, she must be pretty special to turn your head."

I argued, "Since when did you become a relationship expert?"

He laughed and leaned against a wall. "I'm CEO now. It's
my job to give people advice every single day. Romantic
relationships are no different from working relationships."

Summers laughed at that and slapped Will's arm. "I'd love
to see what your secretary thinks of that statement."

Will frowned and opened his mouth to clarify but Ryan held
up his arm to stop him. Ruth ran over with a blue dress held
up proudly in her hands. "What do you think of this one? It
has bows on the straps!"

We ooo'ed and aaa'ed at the dress and she threw it in the
cart I was leaning against. She ran back down the aisle and I
followed slowly.

"What about you Summers? How's Reese?" I shot him a
look.

He coolly looked over his shoulder. "What about Reese? Stone is the one who dated her."

"Right. And you're the one that's been in love with her," Nick added.

Ryan scowled and slapped his shoulder too. He was awfully touchy today. "We're friends. I hang out with her when I'm in town, that's all."

God, is that what I sounded like when I denied being into Georgia? He sounded so pathetic it hurt. But Will, Nick, and I shared looks and left it at that. Ryan and Reese had been playing this game for nearly ten years. Something had to give eventually.

Ryan slapped Will on the back. "What about you, Rose? Got any hot secretaries?"

Will bristled. "To be clear, I don't have relationships with any of my staff. That's unethical and illegal. My secretary is a sixty year old man. But no, I don't have time to do anything other than work and spend time with you losers. And Ruth."

Ryan turned to Nick next who already had his hands up. "Same here. I haven't gone out in months. By the time I'm finished at the restaurant I have no energy to do anything but sleep."

"Well how boring are we? One of us needs to get a girl soon." Summers strutted past me and slapped my back a little too hard. He crouched down next to Ruth and pointed to the shoe section.

Four hours and several hundred dollars later we had a full summer wardrobe for Ruth. She forgot about the gold rings once we got to the mall and I wasn't so eager to remind her about them. We arrived home, said our goodbyes to the three stooges, and went inside.

Ruth started excitedly unpacking all of her new clothes and showing me them as if I hadn't been the one to buy them. I waited through her entire fashion show to ask, "Can we take a nap? I'm tired."

"Can I watch Bluey?" I was willing to do anything for a few minutes of silence at this point. I loved my daughter and friends, but spending hours at a time with everyone always drained me.

"Of course, one episode and that's it though." We curled up on the couch together and I fell asleep before the theme song even started playing.

14

Georgia

I t had been a full week since I met with Reese, Ashton, Ruth and Nick at Reid's diner. Reese and I made plans to hang out last Friday, but she had to stay late at school to empty out her classroom before summer began. I told her no worries, if anything I was relieved to have more writing time. I was really starting to hit my groove.

So we ended up rescheduling for today. I anxiously got ready, I was wearing a summery sundress with strappy sandals and even curled my hair. I looked hotter for Reese than I had for a man in a long time. My nerves got the best of me so I laid down on my bed and anxiously twisted a ring.

I forced myself to take deep breaths and calm the hell down. I was getting worked up over a school teacher that wore polka dot dresses and cat earrings. Reese had been nothing but nice and welcoming so I had nothing to worry about. Hopefully.

As her car pulled in my driveway I stepped away from the window and went to grab my keys and purse. Do I go out to her? Will she text me she's here? What is the protocol? I stood

111

frozen until there was a knock on my door. Thank God.

"Hey! Are you ready?" Reese sounded chipper as always. I held up my purse and keys and turned my back to her to lock the door. I was willing to leave it unlocked when I was home. But no one was going to steal my cat.

"Ready! And very excited." I honestly was. Despite my nerves I was giddy over having a new friend and the promise of plants.

She led me to her car and we both sat down in the front. "Have you eaten yet? Do you want to do lunch or plants first?"

She started pulling out of my driveway while I considered the options. "Maybe we do lunch first? The plants might start dying in the hot car if we leave them for too long."

Her hand slapped the steering wheel. She spoke with a smile, "This is why you're the plant expert and I'm not. I never would have thought of that."

We laughed and she turned on a playlist of hits from the 2000's. She offered to let me choose but I explained how uneducated I was musically. She could have put on Bach or Justin Bieber and it wouldn't have made much of a difference to me.

While we filled our bellies with Thai food, Reese and I talked about ourselves. Not in an interview type of way thankfully. The conversation flowed naturally. But I learned that she had a strained relationship with her parents growing up and I totally related to that. She also let me know she taught English. That perked my ears up.

"I've been tutoring Ruth here and there until she goes to elementary school next year. Ashton tried out daycare at one point but Ruth was just miserable." She slurped up more noodles. Then she sighed out of relief, "She's been going to

112

sports clubs with kids her age in the meantime so hopefully she gets more comfortable." Reese twirled her chopsticks around a noodle as if she was trying to figure it out.

I intercepted the thought, "She's a great kid. I'm sure she'll be just fine." Ashton mentioned that Ruth was slow to trust strangers but she warmed up to me pretty quickly. I thought that there was a chance they were underestimating her ability to adapt.

Reese smiled at me. "She really is. And she has an entire team of volleyball players behind her if she ever needs help."

I laughed and imagined the team of giants escorting Ruth through the halls of elementary school. I spoke softly, "I'm glad she has so many people looking out for her. She's a lucky kid."

Reese agreed and we turned back to our food.

As we walked through the doors of the plant shop my jaw dropped. Reese turned to take in my face and snickered. I was totally expecting a tiny plant store with only a few house plant options. But this was practically house plant heaven.

My shocked face turned to Reese. "This is amazing."

Her smile was bright. "Isn't it? The minute you said you like plants I knew I had to bring you here. It's spectacular even to me and I'm only a novice."

She followed me through the aisles of plants. We created a routine. Reese would pick up a plant that she thought looked cool. And if I recognized it I would tell her how difficult or easy it would be to care for. Once my hands were filled with three plant pots only twenty minutes in, Reese turned around and left me.

She returned with a cart. "We're probably going to need this." I laughed and placed the plants in the cart. I offered to push while we continued on.

The selection of this place was insane. There were so many plants that I had dreamed of having and was never able to find in the city. The cart quickly filled up with at least ten different variations of pothos, philodendrons, and calatheas.

I paused. "Wait, is it okay if I put this in your car? What if they tip over and spill?"

She laughed. "I put a tarp in the back so we're all good to go. Shop to your heart's desire."

We made our way to an outside covered area where bigger plants were housed. I came across a giant monstera and gasped. Reese walked up next to me.

"We're getting this one aren't we?" Her smile was devilish.

I turned back to the plant. It was gorgeous. I had a few monsteras at my old apartment but none had ever gotten this big. I started back tracking, "It probably won't fit in your car. I can come back for one another time."

She put her hand on my arm to stop me. "No, no, no, you looked at that thing like it was your first born child. We are totally getting it."

I looked at her with guilt. She probably wasn't expecting to fit an entire jungle in her car when we first made plans to hang out. She bent down to the plant and tried to lift but it didn't budge.

"Man, that thing is heavy." I bent down with her and we were able to lift it to the bottom section of the cart. It was a little cramped but we only needed it to sit there for a few more minutes.

We went to the checkout and I insisted on paying for Reese's new neon pothos plant. If she was going to have to deal with her car filled to the brim with leaves because of me, this was the least I could do.

I rolled the cart out to the car and we decided to lift the giant monstera in first. After that we played a game of tetris until all the other plants fit in the back, leaving one. I offered, "I'll just carry this one up front with us."

Reese gently closed the trunk and we got back in the car. She turned to me smiling. "This was the most fun I've had in a while. Encouraging you to spend money on plants is my new favorite guilty pleasure. Now I get to enjoy them without having to take care of them."

I laughed and relaxed back in my seat. "If yours starts to die, let me know and I'll take it in as a rescue plant."

She laughed and agreed. "So you haven't told me much about your book yet. Just that you're nonstop writing and chained to your desk because of it."

I gave her a run down of what topics I was covering in it. She seemed interested and sighed. "I would love to write a book one day. Maybe I could start writing this summer."

"You should. What's it like to have summers off? Sounds like a dream."

She pulled her sunglasses down over her eyes as we turned onto a new street. "It's amazing. I don't know how I would survive if I had to go back to working a regular job."

I checked my phone to see if I missed any messages while we were out. It read four o'clock and I was shocked at the fact we spent almost five hours together. "So you've been hanging out a lot with Ashton?"

There was the question I was waiting for. Reese and Ashton were friends so I had no clue how to go about this. "Sort of, we mostly hang out with Ruth around. And he's nice enough to bring me food sometimes when I'm in a writing frenzy."

Ashton had brought me food a few times in the past week. Some of which was from Reid's diner I guessed when one morning I ate some very familiar blueberry pancakes. Another day he brought me the tacos from the Mexican place I raved about after we watched Willy Wonka. I was right before, those were the best tacos.

The only time I stopped writing to leave the house was when I had an idea. Ruth really seemed to enjoy Charlie and the Chocolate Factory before she fell asleep so I went to a bookstore outside of town and picked up a copy. Turns out Rosewood didn't have any bookstores.

I knocked on Ashton's door that afternoon and gave it to him. Thankfully Ruth was taking a nap so she didn't know it was me. But I asked him to try reading it for her. He gave me a smile that rocked my world and asked if I wanted to come in. Writing came first, so I told him I would another time and went back home.

Reese's staring brought me back to reality. "Do you like him?"

"Of course I do, he's Ashton. How could anyone not like him?" She chuckled at the annoyance in my tone.

"He is very charming. I've never seen him look at anyone the way he looks at you." She had a dreamy smile on her face as she spoke.

I was not prepared to sort through whatever the hell that meant so I turned the subject back to her. "Are you dating anyone?"

She huffed. "No, I am very much single. And I plan to stay that way for all of summer."

I quirked an eyebrow at her. "Did something happen?"

She hesitated but continued. "I dated one of the guys on

the volleyball league. We just weren't right for each other but now it's awkward when everyone hangs out. I absolutely hate feeling awkward."

"Oh, was it Ryan?" Her eyes widened to the size of saucers so I tried to self-correct. "He's one of the only people I remember, sorry."

She relaxed a little at that. Then she said regretfully, "No, it was Clay. The firefighter? He's very kind but he's serious and moody. And not capable of letting down any walls."

"Yeah, I can't imagine you with someone like that. You're very open and fun, you need someone to compliment you." My words were honest. Reese and I had bonded throughout the day so I felt like I knew her decently well. She gave me a genuine smile.

"I'm glad to hear that from the relationship expert."

I laughed obnoxiously. "I'm no expert, that's just my humble opinion."

We quieted down and listened to music the last few minutes of the car ride. Parked in the driveway, we hopped out and walked to the trunk to start grabbing plants.

Almost all of the plants were in my house by the time Ashton's truck pulled up. Reese and I were working on the monstera together. We lifted it up from the trunk and began to hobble together when I heard Ashton shouting.

He jogged over with Ruth following. "Easy, there. Put this down please."

Reese and I looked at each other and rolled our eyes. She answered first with the confidence of a lion, "We are strong independent women and we don't need your help Reid."

Seeing the two interact again, I was reminded of how similar they were. It made sense that they were friends for so many years. Reese and Ashton could practically be siblings with their matching confidence and stubborn nature.

We took another step. I was walking backward and Reese forward as she guided me to the porch. She let out a yelp. Then quietly added, "Okay, can we put it down for a second? My hands are slipping."

I helped her gently set it down before Ashton swooped in and lifted it like a sack of potatoes. "Where do you want it?" He called over his shoulder.

Us three girls stood for a minute while Ruth giggled and Reese bit her tongue. I led the charge to follow Ashton inside and pointed to a corner in my sunroom. He set it down gently and turned it so the leaves were facing the light.

His playful smile felt like home. "It's a south facing window right? So the plants will have sun all day."

My eyebrows scrunched. Since when did Ashton know anything about plants? I nodded and thanked him. He started grabbing other plants that Reese and I placed on my coffee table in the living room and asking where they should go.

Reese leaned on the front door frame and gave me a knowing smile. She waved. "I've gotta head out. I promised Ryan I would buy him dinner for helping me move my classroom last week."

I followed her to her car and said goodbye. She went in for a hug so I reciprocated. I took that as a sign this whole friendship outing was a success. I smiled brightly as I thanked her again and told her to drive safely.

We were interrupted by a shrieking Ruth running up to the car. "Wait! Reese, you have to see my new clothes. Uncle Nick and Ryan helped me pick them out. And daddy too, but mostly Uncle Nick."

14

Reese laughed and let Ruth take her hand to pull her toward her house. I decided to go back into mine to find Ashton staring at the remaining plants on the table. "Where's Ruth?"

"She brought Reese to your house to show her some new clothes. Apparently you didn't help too much with picking them out." He scowled playfully.

I reached for a plant and his hand shot out to brush against mine as he stole it from me. He stared at the cleavage my sundress showed as he spoke. "How have you been? Sorry we haven't seen you much. Ruth's swim classes started up again and I've been training hard to prepare for this upcoming charity match."

I looked at his bicep out of confusion. This was his version of out of shape? He looked like the pinnacle of fitness to me. "I've just been writing as usual. I finally hit my groove though so it doesn't feel like I'm constantly starting and stopping to research anymore."

He lifted the plant and raised his eyebrows to ask where it should go. I pointed to the kitchen. "That's great. How much longer do you think it'll be?"

I sighed. "A few weeks? I'm a quarter of the way finished but I'll still need to go back and make edits to it when I'm done."

He nodded and stepped closer after setting the pothos down on the windowsill. He was very close. Almost chest to chest. His eyes returned back to my dress and I wondered what it would feel like to press myself against him. I wanted those strong arms to lift me up and push my back against the wall.

Ruth ran in quickly. Ashton backed up faster and leaned against the counter to put even more space between us.

"Daddy, Reese said my shoes remind her of outer space!" She announced.

119

He glanced my way. The heat in his eyes told me we would finish this later.

15

Ashton

I loved my daughter, but Ruth's timing was dreadful. After a week of seeing Georgia for less than ten minutes in total, I was dying for alone time with her. Instead of thinking less about Georgia since I was seeing her less, my body felt like it was in withdrawal. My hands kept seeking her out everytime she was close to me.

It certainly didn't help to see her in that fucking dress. She looked like my favorite wet dream. Her tits were framed perfectly by the sweet little neck line that was shaped like a heart. I couldn't stop staring at her. I just wanted to bunch up the fabric around her waist and bend her over to see what she was wearing under it.

When I pulled up to see Georgia and Reese trying to lift that ridiculously big plant I was relieved that she was out of her house. I was beginning to worry about her working so much. Everyone has a breaking point and I wanted to make sure Georgia avoided that at all costs.

Reese pulled me out of my thoughts when she announced

she was leaving again. I waved and Georgia walked her to the door to say goodbye.

When she returned Ruth had taken over directing me as to where each plant would look best. I shot her a look to ask if it was okay and she shot me a smile in return. Once Ruth had finished interior decorating, she plopped down on the sofa like she'd just finished a hard days' worth of work.

Georgia sat down next to her. "What have you guys been up to today?"

"We went to practice and it was a conditioning day so it was really boring." Georgia looked up at me in surprise. I wasn't sure if she was shocked over the fact that my five year old knew the term conditioning or if she herself wasn't aware of what it was.

Ruth suddenly sat up and looked around. "Where is Tweet?"

"She's in the backyard. I didn't want her to run out the front door while we were bringing the plants in." Ruth stood up and made her way to the sliding glass door.

She turned to me. "Can I go play with her?"

"I'm not sure how you play with a cat but sure. Go for it." I answered.

Georgia began picking up plants that Ruth arranged and moving them to where she wanted. I recognized some of them from her blogs that I read. She picked up one of the few I recognized. "That's a rattlesnake calathea right? They're the ones that close up when it gets dark. Can I see it sometime?"

She looked shocked. "Since when were you so interested in plants?"

I wasn't sure whether to tell her the truth or not. Stalking the blogs I knew she wrote could definitely come off as creepy. And I certainly didn't want to scare her away. But I couldn't think of any other possible explanation.

I explained awkwardly, "I might have read a little about them online. There's this really neat blog that writes about plants, Pothos and Vine." Her eyes widened and her head tilted like a confused puppy.

She set the plant down and walked closer to me. With wide eyes she asked, "You read my stuff?"

Well the cat was out of the bag now. Might as well own up to all of it. "Yeah, I read all the ones you mentioned. The cooking, plants, and even relationship advice blog. It was very informative."

"I didn't know you would actually read it. I can't believe you did that." The shock in her voice was evident. We held eye contact as she took another step closer. I couldn't stop my hand from holding her elbow and tracing up her arm.

I smiled and leaned my head down until we were almost nose to nose. I spoke softly now. "Of course I did. And I have to say your writing is way better than your baking."

She did a cute little laugh and her nose scrunched up. I bumped our noses together and the corners of my eyes crinkled as my smile grew even bigger. She took a shallow breath and glanced down at my lips.

Ruth shrieked and the sunroom door slid open. I jumped back still holding Georgia's elbow. Not again. Ruth screamed, "Tweet jumped over the fence!"

Georgia pulled away and quickly followed Ruth outside. I took a second to breathe and stare at the ceiling. Never had I worked so hard for a damn kiss. I joined them outside to see Georgia running over to our backyard and chasing after a cat.

I jogged over and together we cornered the cat against the back of my house. Georgia scooped her up and gave her a stern talking to before we all headed back inside.

"I think she has magical powers! She was sitting on the trash can and jumped so high over the fence! It's like this tall." Ruth stood on her tippy toes and stretched her hand as high as it would go.

Georgia let out a breathy laugh and set the cat down. "She's definitely an escape artist."

She gave me an apologetic look and I was too selfish to take Ruth and go home. I asked hopefully, "Have you had dinner yet?"

Georgia shook her head. "Nope. Reese and I had Thai for lunch in the next town over. But no dinner yet."

I looked at Ruth and leaned down to whisper in her ear. "Do you want to invite her over for dinner?" I got a very excited nod in return.

She reached for my hand and we both turned to Georgia. "How would you like to have dinner over at the Reid's tonight? Not Reid's diner but you know our house. With just us two." I sounded like a goddamn moron.

Georgia laughed anyway. "Thanks for clarifying. I would love to."

I offered Ruth a high five with my free hand and she slapped her own hand down on it. She smiled brightly at Georgia and went to grab her hand to drag her over to our house.

We made the quick walk over and I swung open my fridge door to take stock of what we had. It wasn't too empty. Ruth dragged Georgia upstairs to show off her new closet while I quickly pulled up a recipe that was bookmarked on my phone.

16

Georgia

After Ruth gave me a thorough explanation of every new piece of clothing she got from her shopping spree, we headed back downstairs. Smelling basil and lemon I headed into the kitchen to see what Ashton was up to. Ruth climbed up on her step stool to look at what he was doing too.

"What's this?" She asked.

"I'm making some lemon basil pesto pasta." He shot me a look.

I bit my lip and watched him chop up some basil. "Trying out a new recipe?"

He proudly smiled back. "Yeah, it should be pretty good. It's from this food blog I've really been enjoying lately."

I snickered. Ruth's face scrunched up and she asked, "What's a food blog?"

I answered for him. "It's sort of like the cookbook we used. But it's online."

She nodded, satisfied with my answer. I reached for a lemon

and the grater sitting next to it. "Want some help?"

He looked me over. His heated gaze made my cheeks flush. He spoke confidently, "No, I'm trying to prove I can cook a solid meal alone. Ruth, do you want to teach Georgia how to play go fish?"

When Ashton was satisfied with his dinner he called us back into the kitchen. The table was set and I looked down at the dishes that were set out. They were plated beautifully and it looked like he even grated fresh parmesan on top.

"Wow, this looks amazing. Thank you." I waited for Ruth to sit first. The table had three chairs and I wasn't sure where they normally sat.

Ashton saw my hesitation and came over to pull out the chair across from Ruth for me. "What do you want to drink? We've got water, juice, milk, or beer."

"Water's good. Thanks." I sat down. Ashton grabbed two glasses of water and set a juice box in front of Ruth.

Ashton finally sat too as Ruth pushed pasta around with her fork. "Is it supposed to be green?"

He snorted. "Yes, lemon drop. It's pesto pasta, the basil is what makes it green. Taste it. It's really good."

She tried a bite cautiously. Ashton and I waited in silence for her reaction. She chewed and swallowed before wiggling happily in her chair. Ashton's face broke out in a grin and he looked down at his plate to get a forkful of his own pasta.

I took that as my cue to dive in too. It really was delicious. Ashton had cooked the pasta perfectly and there wasn't too much lemon either. He really did read my blog post to make it exactly how I like it.

I tried to remember the last time anyone had cooked for me.

16

My sister Arden brought me baked bread and pastries all the time when we lived near each other, but she wasn't much of a cook.

Actually, I couldn't remember a time when anyone had ever treated me the way Ashton did. Even in my past relationships, boyfriends never brought me food or lattes unless it was for a special occasion. Much less every day.

"Do you like it?" Ashton asked. I was so caught up in thinking about him I nearly forgot he was sitting right next to me.

I took a sip of water and nodded. "It's amazing. So the Reid's are known for volleyball and cooking?"

He laughed. Ruth quickly corrected me. "Uncle Nick is good at cooking. I'm pretty good too."

Ashton shook his head and shoved another bite in his mouth. "Well your dad seems to be pretty great too. It must be a Reid thing."

She looked over at him as if she was seeing him in a new light. She took another bite and chewed thoughtfully before answering. "Yeah maybe it is."

I smiled and Ashton gave me a look of disbelief. I bit my lip and looked down at my food to hide my goofy smile. His ankle crossed under mine beneath the table and rested there until we finished dinner.

Ruth told me all about her swim lessons at the local pool. According to Ashton she was the best one there even though she was the youngest. She had even graduated to a pool noodle and no longer needed floaties.

"Can we watch another movie together?" Ruth asked while Ashton got up to move our dirty dishes. I looked to Ashton, more than willing to let him answer this one.

"Georgia, do you want to stay for a movie?" I would pluck

127

out my own eyelashes one by one if it meant I got to spend more time with them.

A thought struck me. "Sure, but I did think of a book that Ruth might like. What if I read it for you guys instead?"

Ashton looked to Ruth for approval. She surprisingly nodded without hesitation. "We almost finished Charlie and the Chocolate Factory. Daddy reads it in all of their voices."

I laughed and stood up. "Can I help with the dishes?"

I got a very nasty look from Ashton. "Hell no, peach. Sit down please."

My eyes rolled on their own and I remained on my feet. "I'll just go grab the book then. Be right back."

Book in hand, I walked back inside Ashton's house to find Ashton and Ruth washing dishes. He was washing and she was using a dish towel to dry while standing on her little step stool next to him. I stayed quiet and leaned against the door frame.

Ruth was chirping about the green pasta for dinner and asked Ashton if he could make other colors of pasta like blue or purple. He promised to find a recipe one day for them to make together. Watching them do something as simple as watching dishes made my heart want to burst.

Ruth saw me first when she was stepping down from her stool. "You're back! Do you have the book?"

I held it up for her to see. "I'm ready if you are." She took my hand and led me to the living room.

We sat down on the couch and got comfy. "Wait, we need blankets."

Ruth ran upstairs and came back with two blankets. Ashton joined us and they sat down on the couch next to me with Ruth in the middle. I scooted close to her so she could see the book since there were some pictures in it.

128

"Okay you two, these are the Sideways Stories from Wayside School. Everyone comfy?" I looked at Ashton over Ruth's head. He slouched a little more into the couch and wrapped his arm along the back of the couch so his hand rested on my shoulder.

Ruth answered. "Ready!"

I started reading and didn't stop until I noticed Ruth's eyelids blinking very slowly. I looked up from the book for the first time. "Is it bedtime?"

Ashton sat up and pulled his arm away from me. "I think so. Come on lady bug, let's get ready for bed."

He carried a very sleepy Ruth upstairs and I wandered back into the kitchen. I noticed there were some other dishes still in the sink that they hadn't cleaned. So I got to work and started scrubbing pots and pans.

Ashton returned downstairs. I asked him where everything went and he took the pot from my hands to start putting things away himself. "Thank you, you didn't have to do that."

"You made dinner. I wanted to help out too." He shot me a smile from where he was bent putting a pan away.

This was probably the appropriate time to leave. Although I really wasn't ready to yet. Before I could voice my thoughts Ashton spoke.

"So one of my old teammates is playing a match today on TV. I was going to watch it, it starts in a few minutes. Do you wanna join?" Thank God. The last time we were alone was in his kitchen at night just like this weeks ago. It had been too long.

I nodded. "Yeah, that'd be great. I can impress you with my new volleyball knowledge thanks to Ruth."

He laughed and opened the fridge. He grabbed a beer, opened it, and offered it to me. "Want one?"

"Yeah sure, thanks." I took it and followed him into the living room.

He fished for the remote between the couch cushions and invited me to sit next to him. The TV was turned on to the game. "So which one is your friend?"

"He plays for the Giants. Number 13." I focused on the game again.

Ashton's hand found its way to my shoulder again as he stretched over the back of the couch. I couldn't help but breathe out a laugh at how cliche it was. He turned to glare at me playfully.

"You got a problem over there peach?" His playful smile drew my eyes to his lips. How many times had we almost kissed today? This was beginning to feel like torture.

I shook my head and turned it right back to the TV screen. "No problems. So if he isn't a setter what position does he play?"

"Who said he wasn't a setter?" He asked.

I looked at him again. "Well no one, but you said you played together. There can only be one setter right?"

One of his eyebrows raised. "Ruth told you I'm a setter?"

Oh, shit. I totally just gave myself away. He noticed my awkward pause. Then a smirk replaced his smile. "Did you look me up?"

I rolled my eyes and scoffed. "No, well sort of. I watched some of your games from the Olympics."

That really made his eyebrows raise. He set his beer down on the table in front of us and turned his entire body to face me. One of his hands smoothly landed on my knee while his other arm remained around my shoulders. He eagerly asked, "You watched me play? When?"

I took a sip of my beer to distract myself. The full weight of his attention made my stomach flutter. Defensively I answered, "I was curious. Being an Olympian is sort of a big deal so I looked you up after you told me that night."

He continued to keep his eyes on me. I took another nervous sip. Using his arm that wasn't wrapped around my shoulder, he grabbed my beer and set it on the table too. His eyes returned to mine and this time I didn't look away.

He glanced down at my lips and his hand came up to hold the side of my jaw. The warm hand on my neck encouraged goosebumps to bloom on my skin. I forgot to breathe and focused on his mouth. His nose nudged mine and I leaned in.

This was the closest I had ever felt to euphoria. I waited for this for so long my brain fully shut off and I was only acting on instinct. Ashton Reid felt like a drug and I was a very willing addict.

His lips brushed mine and paused. I took charge and pressed our lips together firmly. Faster than I could react, he slid his hand behind my neck and pulled me as close as possible while he kissed me breathless.

My hands rose to grip his shirt and pull him even closer. His hand slid down my thigh beneath the hem of my dress to pull my leg over his lap. He separated our lips for a split second to breathe and I snapped back to reality. My entire body froze.

He pulled back even more when he felt my body tense. "You okay?"

His hand softly gripped my thigh as he focused on my face. I whispered, "Yeah. Yeah, I'm good."

So many thoughts were going through my brain at once I couldn't keep up. The common denominator between all of the thoughts was one feeling; *panic*. There was my book and my career to think about. And the fact that he was Ashton freaking Reid and my neighbor.

I can't date my neighbor. What if we broke up and I would have to live through seeing him bring home other women for the rest of my goddamn life? Or worse, what if I had to watch him fall in love. And Ruth. If we dated and broke up that would ruin my relationship with her too.

"Are you sure? Because you look very not good right now." He sounded worried. His eyes were looking right into my damn soul. And I knew at that moment, if I did this I would never go a day in my life without thinking about Ashton Reid again.

I shot up off of the couch. "Yeah, I just- I need to go."

I looked around for my purse. Had I brought my purse over? Ashton stopped me with a gentle hand on my wrist. "Hey, easy peach. I'm sorry, did you not want-"

"No! No, that's not it. I did, I do want this. But not right now. I've got my book and I just moved here. And we're *neighbors*," I nervously rambled. Ashton looked both horrified and amused.

He forced out a laugh. "You don't want me to kiss you because we're *neighbors*?"

I dropped my head and pinched the bridge of my nose. "No, I mean yes. I do want this but what if it doesn't work out? I really need to focus on my book right now. This is the biggest moment of potentially my entire career. And you have your charity match right?"

He nodded. "Okay, so not right now."

"Not right now." I repeated. Who was I kidding, a man like Ashton was never going to wait for a loser like me to be ready for... Whatever it was we were about to start on that couch.

He took a deep breath and sighed. "I can do that. We can

16

still be friends for now right?"

I nodded quickly. "Of course. I would really love that."

"Okay, then. Do you want to watch the game? I promise I can keep my hands to myself." He raised his hands up as proof.

I laughed and led the way back to the living room. "I really am sor-"

"Peach, do not apologize to me for not wanting to jump in head first. We'll go at your pace. There is absolutely nothing to apologize for." His stern dad voice was not helping my situation.

Half of me screamed that I should just jump in his lap and continue where we left off. But the other much more cautious half had been running the show for the last few decades. So I listened to that voice instead.

He threw me another look. "Here, take the blanket. Get comfy cozy."

Hearing Ashton say the phrase comfy cozy was endearing enough to distract me from panicking. I listened to his orders and snuggled into the couch as close as possible to him without touching.

133

17

Ashton

My heart raced after I replayed Georgia's reaction to our kiss over and over again in my mind. That kiss was mind blowing. I felt like I went to a different dimension and back. There were fireworks exploding behind my eyes.

And I knew she felt it too. During the kiss she was just as desperate as I was and damn near ripped my shirt pulling me closer. She kissed me back with just as much passion as I gave her. But then I broke it and she froze up.

I was glad she explained her perspective. She asked to take things slow which reminded me I didn't know much about Georgia's past dating history. We were around the same age and Ruth said she'd had a few boyfriends before so I knew she wasn't completely inexperienced.

Keeping my hands to myself wouldn't be easy. But at this point I was willing to become a born again virgin to keep seeing Georgia. Every moment of silence I had lately, my head filled with thoughts of her. Just like now.

She looked so sweet with a strap of her dress half fallen off of her shoulder. The sweetheart neckline gave me a perfect view of her tits but I forced myself to look away. I squeezed my eyes shut to blink away the thoughts of temptation.

I looked down again at her head resting on my shoulder. She was covered with a blanket and her legs were folded under her. She fell asleep at some point during the match and I wasn't sure what to do. I promised to keep my hands to myself, but I knew she had lost sleep lately to keep writing.

I shifted my shoulder that she was resting on and sat up a little. "Hey, peach."

She snuggled even further into my shoulder. I spoke softly, "Come on. Let's go get you in bed."

The sound that came from her mouth was entirely unintelligible. I helped her sit up and slipped my arm around her back to help her up the stairs. Even standing, her eyes were barely open.

We made our way up the stairs slowly and I laid her down on my bed with her legs hanging off. I bent down on one knee to undo the buckles on her strappy sandals and set them near the bedside table. Then I shifted her legs to rest on the bed too and pulled the comforter over her.

"Goodnight, peach." I flipped the light switch and closed the door behind me. In the downstairs closet I pulled out an extra blanket and pillow to make my bed on the couch. After setting it up I laid down and fell asleep thinking of ways to show Georgia I could make her happier than anyone else.

Birds chirping woke me up early the next morning. I sat up quickly, remembering what happened last night. My phone clock read six a.m. Ruth would wake up soon which meant I should probably go wake up Georgia. I didn't want to wake her up at six but that seemed like the safest option for both Ruth and Georgia.

I sat up and ran a hand through my hair and down over my face. This was going to be a long morning. Rising to my feet, I decided to take today one step at a time. And I hoped that Georgia wasn't upset about sleeping over last night.

I crept up the stairs and slowly pushed open my bedroom door. The sight in front of me was not at all what I expected. My room was empty and the bed was made. There were no shoes left by the nightstand. Was I hallucinating last night? If so, it was the sweetest dream of my life.

I checked the bathroom and made my way back downstairs. The kitchen was empty. Dining room was empty too. I doubled back to the living room and it was still the way I left it. I was half tempted to run over to Georgia's house to make sure she was okay. But if she snuck out like that, her sleeping over must have been worse than I thought.

Ruth's bedroom door creaked open and she called down the stairs. "Daddy, what are you doing? The sun isn't up?"

I headed back upstairs. "Just getting some water. Let's go back to bed."

"Can I come sleep with you?" She rubbed her sleepy eyes with the back of her hand.

"Sure, pumpkin. Come on." I climbed into bed and held out my arm for her.

We dozed off again in the early morning and I smelled lavender on my pillow case. When I woke up a few hours later I had a text from Georgia. 'Sorry I left so early. I woke up and couldn't go back to sleep but didn't want to wake you. Thanks for last night. I had a fun time x.'

18

Georgia

I woke up at five o'clock in the morning in someone else's bed. It took me a minute to remember where I was as my hands ran along the soft silk sheets. When I remembered I sat up so fast I had to blink away stars in my eyes. I was in Ashton's bed. And he was… on the couch?

We kissed last night. And not just a quick kiss. That was the best kiss of my entire life. He grabbed me and held on like kissing me was as necessary as breathing. But then I ruined it by asking him to wait. I am such a moron.

I looked around for my shoes and quickly slipped them on when I found them. With my phone planted firmly in my pocket I decided to flee now rather than face the awkward morning after. I tiptoed down the stairs as quietly as possible and walked past Ashton passed out on the couch.

When I reached the front door I realized I didn't have a key to lock it back behind me. I couldn't leave the house unlocked in the dark. I headed to the back door and hoped it was like mine and could be shut while locked. Success! My phone flashlight came in handy as I crossed our backyards to open my fence gate and head inside my house.

My bed looked cold. Tweet at least welcomed me home by brushing against my legs. I peeled off my clothes from yesterday and shrugged on a big t-shirt before getting in bed. No matter how hard I tried I could not fall back asleep.

Maybe I should have left a note telling him that I left. What if he woke up and wondered where I was? I couldn't text him now. It was still only fifteen after five. I set an alarm for 8 o'clock and decided to text him then.

I reached over to my night stand to grab my laptop. I opened up my schedule that included the timeline of how long I had to write my book. It was full. I was really going to have to focus to get all of the writing done in time and still have extra days to edit.

The next three weeks would be crunch time. I had exactly three weeks and three days left to create a fully polished book worthy enough for thousands of people to enjoy. It was even more pressure that it wasn't being published under my name. The last thing I wanted was to make my client look bad.

I vowed to myself that I would only focus on my book these next few weeks. I had an entire lifetime to worry about men. Writing this book might be the only chance I had to prove my writing skills worthy.

When my alarm finally went off I texted Ashton and apologized for leaving so early. Then I called my sister. I sighed in anticipation, she was not going to like this but I really needed to focus on my book. I wanted total isolation until I finished it

She answered the phone with a yawn. "What's up?"

"Hey, I'm running a little behind schedule on my book so

I won't be able to come visit next weekend. I really need to hunker down and focus."

She quietly laughed. "As if you aren't focused enough. Don't you have a few weeks left? You seriously can't wait for a couple of days? I'll even let you bring your laptop."

My head shook even though she couldn't see me. "No, I'm sorry. After I'm done I'll come and visit and we can celebrate. Sounds good?"

She let out a long sigh. "Georgia what's going on?"

"What do you mean?"

"You're avoiding me. And canceling plans over a week away. You could catch up on your writing in that time so what's the real reason?"

I rubbed the ring on my pointer finger with my thumb. "I'm just stressing out. This is the first time I've ever written a book and I want it to be good."

"So this has nothing to do with the hot neighbor you told me about?"

I paused. Lying to my sister was not a habit that I wanted to get into. This was mostly about the book. Almost entirely. But there was a small part of me that was perhaps a teensy bit terrified by the idea of Ashton Reid wanting me.

"He's great. I just saw him yesterday." Technically not a lie. "I won't have time to hang out with him either. I just want to focus on the book." Totally not a lie.

Unless I was lying to myself. But that was a problem for future me to deal with. My sister hummed and I heard a door slam in the background.

"Hey Georg, I've gotta go. But please call me if you change your mind."

"I will. Love you, bye." I hung up and let my head fall back to my pillow. There was no way I was going to change my mind.

Two weeks passed by quickly when every day looked the exact same. First, my alarm went off and I went through my morning routine. Next, I brewed a pot of coffee and drank it while reviewing my notes for upcoming chapters I needed to write. Then, I sat at the chair in front of my desk until my growling stomach refused to be ignored.

The only thing that broke my routine occasionally was Ashton. He hadn't stopped bringing me food or lattes. And now he even started adding little notes to the bags of food he left at my doorstep.

Yesterday's note was scribbled in red ink. I picked it up from where I had them all stacked on my kitchen counter. My place was a complete wreck.

The note read: 'Ruth made sure to scream heads up anytime Johnson served at practice today. We finished reading Sideways Stories. She wanted to read it with you but I convinced her that if we finished this book you would have to bring us the next in the series. I hope writing is going well. x Ashton'

I started flipping through the other notes to read through them but a knock interrupted me. I checked my phone for the time. They must be leaving breakfast for me today. I waited a minute for Ashton and Ruth to have time to run home before I opened my door.

I turned the door knob and was suddenly faced with my sister. My entire body froze. I hoped if I didn't move maybe she hadn't seen my 5'10 frame standing right smack in front of her.

"Good to know you're alive." Arden was pissed. She was standing in my home and looked pissed which was so much worse.

140

"What are you doing here? Did something happen?" She stormed past me to look around.

"Yes, my baby sister went rogue. Why do you have take out boxes everywhere? And what is this plate doing sitting on the couch?" She asked with venom in her voice. I hung my head in shame.

"Well last night I was writing on my laptop while eating dinner and-" I stopped when I saw her face. That was definitely meant to be a rhetorical question.

She started grabbing boxes and headed to the kitchen. "Arden, you don't need to clean my house."

"Where are the trash bags? You are going to sit right there." She pointed at a stool at the island. "While I clean this place, you are going to tell me what the hell is going on."

I sat down. When Arden was upset there was no reasoning with her. It was best to comply in this situation. I sighed, "Okay, they're under the sink."

She grabbed a trash bag and started shoving everything into it. I quickly stood back up and moved the pile of notes to a drawer before sitting back down.

"Well? Get to talking." She demanded. Great, she wanted a freaking monologue.

"Nothing explicitly happened. Well sort of. But nothing that was a big deal. I guess I just got a little overwhelmed is all." My words trailed off. Arden stood up straight and shoved another take out box in her trash bag.

"Explain." The one word response made me wince.

I twisted the ring on my left middle finger with my right hand. "Well I got a little behind on my book. I made a new friend and we went plant shopping one day which was really fun. And then I was invited to dinner at Ashton's so I went."

She didn't respond and moved to the living room to start throwing away trash there. I spun on my stool so I was still facing her. "And then I ended up having to rewrite an entire chapter because it sounded like complete nonsense."

She made her way through the sunroom and back to the kitchen. "That's it?"

Guilt twisted in my gut. "Ashton kissed me. Like full on kissed me after his daughter went to bed. And I'm sort of freaking out about it so I decided to focus on my book instead." I finally confessed.

The trash bag was carelessly tossed to the floor and she sat down next to me. "Okay, so he likes you. And you clearly like him right?"

I nodded. "Then what is there to freak out about?" She asked.

I slow blinked at her as if that was the dumbest question in the world. It *was* a dumb question. He's Ashton Reid. Way out of my league and he had a daughter and was my next door *neighbor*. But I wasn't sure how to put all of that into words for Arden to understand.

I spoke hesitantly, "He's really nice. And he brings me food and lattes. But not in an overbearing 'you owe me for this' way. In a genuine 'I want to take care of you' kind of way. He doesn't even hand it to me directly, he leaves it on my doorstep and ding dong ditches me." It was Arden's turn to slow blink.

"And that's supposed to be a *bad* thing?"

"No, it's a great thing. A too-great thing almost. He's way out of my league. Actually, I think you two would be perfect together. He's confident and overly caring like you are." The thought of my sister and Ashton together made my stomach even more sick.

142

I was halfway to vomiting when Arden spoke again. "So you're worried he's too good for you?"

"Yes, obviously. Did I tell you he played in the Olympics? And he has the coolest daughter on the planet. And he has like a million friends that all care about him and Ruth so much."

"Ruth is his daughter?" I nodded. "You do realize you're Georgia Mitchell right?"

I laughed out loud. As if that meant anything to anyone. Arden grabbed my shoulder and yanked me until I faced her. "You are my favorite person on this entire planet. There is not a man on Earth that is too good for you. Do you hear me?"

I nodded and laughed shakily. She continued, "Good, because I'm your big sister and I'm always right. Now get up and go take a shower. I want a tour of town."

"You do realize that I haven't even gotten a tour of town right?" She rolled her eyes and got up to continue cleaning.

"We'll figure it out together then. Now go," She ordered.

I headed upstairs and took a scorching hot shower. By the time my skin was pink from the heat I had finished scrubbing my entire body and washing my hair. I stepped out of the shower and put on a towel to find some clothes to wear.

All of my lounging and comfy clothes were dirty since that was my work attire for the last two weeks. I reached for a flowy dress and finished getting ready. My hair was dry and my lips had a sheer sheen of gloss when I met Arden back downstairs.

She wasn't joking when she said she was going to clean the place. It looked almost back to normal. She looked up at me and snapped, "You're driving. It took me almost two hours to get here and if I have to be behind the wheel for one more minute I'm going to lose it."

I snickered and followed her out the door. My bossy big sister was back which meant she wasn't as pissed anymore. "I'm sorry for going ghost," I added guiltily.

"Don't be. You being in love totally makes up for how angry I was." My eyebrows furrowed. In *love*? I certainly did not remember those words coming out of my mouth.

She sat in my passenger seat and pulled out her phone. "I want ice cream first. Step on the gas Jeeves."

I rolled my eyes. Today was going to be a long day. And my sister was definitely going to make me regret not talking to her sooner about this. I strapped in. Both figuratively and literally as I clicked my seatbelt in and started the car.

19

Ashton

I held tight onto Ruth's hand as we walked to yet another store. We didn't have enough time to drive to the mall outside of town so I decided our best bet was to try every clothing store in downtown Rosewood. Ruth knew I was in one of my rare foul moods so she was thankfully acting easy going today.

These last few weeks were a little difficult. The countdown to kindergarten started and I was determined to help my baby girl feel confident in herself around other kids. Which meant a lot of summer activities. She had swim lessons three times a week, dance class, and most recently soccer. Unfortunately, they didn't have volleyball for kids her age but I would let it slide for now.

She also went to Reese's drama club for summer school kids every week. They were much older than her but Reese offered to watch her while I got some extra training time in. Her club was performing a play for the Wizard of Oz tonight and apparently the older kids convinced Ruth to join. Which was

145

the reason why we were scouring downtown for a pair of green leggings to make her poppy costume.

Between carting Ruth back and forth between her activities and my rigorous training schedule before the charity match, I barely had time to breathe. If I was being honest with myself I was probably working harder than I needed to. It was just a charity match for fun after all. But this was the first game I would play in front of a crowd since Ruth was a baby.

This would be the first experience Ruth would ever remember of her dad playing live right in front of her. And not to mention the fact that I was a pro athlete with my own very high standards. It had been a few years since I played pro but I still had fans that would probably watch. Plus, there was sure to be a very live crowd watching either way.

I hadn't been conditioning or training anywhere near to the level I was when I played pro. We played practice matches in the local league and I still worked out regularly, but that was like having training wheels compared to an actual match in front of a crowd.

I also really wanted to invite Georgia. She sneakily found old footage of my Olympic games. How the hell was I supposed to compete with my past self who lived and breathed volleyball? Now I lived and breathed snacks and swim lessons.

Georgia might not even come. And that was sure as hell a lot worse than her watching me fail miserably. After she declared her 'not right now' rule I was still as smitten as ever. The woman could bring another man home and I would still be watching the clock waiting for her to be ready.

Ruth and I were just about to pass the ice cream shop when the door opened. Georgia walked out smiling with a chocolate ice cream cone in her hand. She was wearing a pretty little green dress that flowed around her in the wind.

When she saw us she stopped so fast the girl behind her nearly smashed into her back. Her jaw dropped and Ruth screamed. "Georgia!"

Georgia's shock turned back into a smile as Ruth abandoned my hand and ran up to her. I tried my best to cool my nerves and smile but I was already a stressed out mess today. My hand found its way to my hair to push it back roughly.

"Hey, Ruth. What a surprise." Georgia wrapped her free arm around Ruth and looked up at me with a shy smile. "Hey, Ashton."

That smile shredded me to pieces in an instant. All of my stress melted away and I was left a smiling idiot. "Hey, you found the ice cream shop." Clearly.

Georgia laughed and the girl behind her stepped next to her to get a good look at me. She smiled but her eyes were serious as she looked back and forth between Georgia, Ruth, and I. "Yeah, my sister came to visit and she demanded ice cream. So here we are."

Her sister elbowed Georgia. "Oh, right. Ashton, Ruth, this is Arden. Arden." She gestured to us. "Ashton and Ruth."

Arden stepped up and offered me her hand. "I have heard so much about you. I'm so glad we could finally meet."

So she did talk about me. Georgia's cheeks immediately heated. She glared at her sister and then looked at Ruth. "What are you guys doing? Getting some ice cream?"

Ruth turned to me as if that was clearly an offer she would take. I gently put my hand over her mouth to stop the thought from being spoken. "Nope, we're looking for some green tights."

My hand was pushed away by a much smaller one. "Daddy,

they're called leggings." She focused her entire attention on Georgia. "I have a play tonight, will you come? It's the Wizard of Oz! And I'm playing a poppy. I just have to stand and dance like a flower would. But I'm kind of nervous."

I was not expecting that. Usually the only person Ruth actively invited or asked to hang out with us was Nick. But I guess Georgia had a big impact on the both of us. "Ruth, Georgia's sister is in town. She probably has plans to hang out with her."

Arden interceded. While shorter than Georgia, she was clearly the more confident sibling. She lacked all of Georgia's cute nervous habits. "Don't worry about me! This was just a day trip. I have work tomorrow so I'll be leaving in a few hours."

The sisters shared a look and Ruth waited for the verdict. "I would love to if that's okay with you?"

Georgia's eyes met mine. Did she really need to ask if I wanted her there? I wasn't sure how to be more clear about the fact that I wanted no one but her to be around for the rest of our lives. "Of course it is."

I tried my best to put on a reassuring smile but felt so damn confused. In what world was there debate about if I wanted her around all of the time. I made a mental note to say it out loud the next time we were alone.

"Yay! I'm so glad! And maybe you can come over after and we can make some cupcakes! Or read again. We finished the book you left us so we need another."

Georgia smiled and bent down to Ruth's level. "We'll see about that after the play. But I will definitely get you a new book as soon as I can."

They shared a high five and we all said our goodbyes. I

148

watched as Georgia walked away and Ruth giggled while pulling my arm to go to the next store.

* * *

I knocked on Georgia's door as the sun was setting. She opened it after a few minutes and I nearly fell to my knees. Her dress was different now. Gold hoop earrings dangled from her ears and it made me want to pull on them. Her cheeks were shimmering and her lips were the most perfect shade of red I'd ever seen.

Everything in me wanted to grab her and mess up those perfectly red lips but I stood still. My daughter's hand in mine grounded me. I forced myself to look away from Georgia. Staring at her was like looking at the sun for too long sometimes. She was so bright and lovely it physically hurt.

Georgia broke the silence first. "Hey, you two look good."

She looked up and down at my button up and slacks and then gave Ruth a smile that wrinkled her nose. "I love your flower costume. You found the leggings I see."

Ruth cheerfully smiled. "We did! And Reese made the flower petals." She reached up to tap the ridiculously big headband on her head that had giant flower petals hot glued onto it.

Ruth reached for Georgia's hand with her free hand. "Come on! We're going to be late."

I realized I hadn't spoken at all yet. "You look great," I breathed out. I made eye contact with her over Ruth's head. "Thanks again for coming with us."

She smiled. "I wouldn't miss it for the world."

Ruth nervously chattered the entire car ride. Mostly to

herself. I was thankful for the noise though because I wasn't sure I could form intelligible thoughts with Georgia looking like that.

Once we arrived at the school we walked Ruth backstage until I spotted Reese's curly hair and waved her over. "Hey! Just in time. Come on flower girl, this is going to be so much fun!"

Reese sounded like she had an entire pot of coffee before this. Ruth paused and squeezed my hand. She looked like a deer in headlights. I realized my girl had never been in front of a crowd before and I remembered my first time playing a real game. Sweat was pouring off my body in buckets.

I kneeled down and looked her in the eyes. "Hey, you've got this. You're a Reid." I patted her shoulder. "We're good at a few things and one of those is entertaining a crowd. This is no different than your dance performances for us at volleyball practices. Just look at me if you get nervous okay?"

She nodded firmly. My heart nearly burst with pride. "Go get 'em tiger."

She giggled. "See ya later alligator!"

Reese grabbed her hand and waved before taking her away from us. I turned to Georgia and offered her my elbow. She linked our arms and I led us back to the seating area. Once again all I could think of was what the fuck to say.

"You clean up well. I wasn't aware you could be so-" She waved her hand gesturing at my body. "Formal."

I laughed. With a glare I asked, "Are you trying to call me scruffy?"

"Not scruffy just relaxed I guess. The first time we met you were wearing sweatpants in a grocery store."

I furrowed my eyebrows. "What's wrong with sweatpants?"

She let out a full laugh from those perfect lips. "Are you laughing at me?"

She cutely covered her mouth with a hand. "No, not at all. You're just not the suit and tie type, that's all."

I playfully squinted at her. "Right, well if you're done insulting me now we should go find our seats."

She tilted her head with a playful smile growing. "I'm not insulting you. You're awfully defensive today."

"I'm a little stressed. Ruth is super nervous and I'm trying to build her confidence before kindergarten starts. We need this play to go well." Her smile turned into a frown.

I wanted to take my thumb, smudge her lipstick, and wipe the frown right off of her face. "I'm sure she'll do great. You raised a great kid and she's a *Reid*." Her finger poked my chest.

I laughed and gestured for her to sit as we found our seats. "You're right."

"So your sister came to visit?" I tried a new topic.

Georgia sighed and shrugged. "Yeah, it was a surprise to me." She looked over at me nervously. "She was a little pissed that I've been hermiting in my house and avoiding everyone."

I nodded and added, "She was worried about you."

"Yeah, and she might have talked a little sense into me. I'm sorry for running off on you like that." She said nervously as she twisted a ring again. I wanted to grab that hand and let her play with my fingers instead.

My forehead wrinkled. "Sorry? For what?"

She looked down at her hands in her lap. "For running. I've never been good at the whole feelings thing." She paused at my snort. "Ironic, I know. But I sort of convinced myself it would be safer to focus on the book before trying to figure out whatever this is."

Her finger pointed back and forth between us. I finally grabbed her hand and entwined our fingers. "Got it. Nothing to be sorry for, peach. We go at your pace. I can be patient. I'm a *Reid,* remember? We almost always get what we want."

And I wanted her. More than anything. So much so I was willing to wait lifetimes if it meant Georgia Mitchell would be mine and I would be hers.

We held eye contact until the stage lights went down and music started playing.

Georgia's hand remained in mine for the entirety of the play. It was as entertaining as a high school play could possibly be. I even snapped a few pictures when Ruth came out to do her 'flower dance'.

The lights turned on again and I let go of her hand. She spoke happily, "That was great! She's going to be so excited."

I returned the smile and nodded. "We'll be hearing about it for years to come."

She laughed and we remained sitting while everyone else rose to exit. "Reese is going to be a while so it's probably best to just wait."

"Okay, how is training going? For your charity match?"

I let out a long breath. Now that the play was over and successful all of my worry turned to my own performance. "It's been a lot. Exhausting. Honestly, I'm a little worried I won't play anywhere near the level I used to play at."

She turned her body to fully face me. "Well, obviously. You said you retired years ago. And you're a single dad. You take care of Ruth full time. Why would you play at the same level?"

Her brutal honesty shocked me. She wasn't wrong though. I stayed silent.

"Would you mind if I came? I could sit with Ruth if you need

152

someone to watch her," She offered.

I turned back to face her. "You would come?"

"Of course I would. I want to see *the* Ashton Reid in action. In his element." She snickered.

"I would love it if you came. And Ruth will be excited to sit with you in the stands." I looked down to see her twisting a ring again. I placed my hand over hers to stop her before I started twisting her ring myself. "You promise not to be disappointed if I suck?"

She laughed and placed her other hand over mine. "Ash, you could go out there and serve the ball right to my face and I would still be amazed. My volleyball standards are very low so just act confident and I will be very impressed."

I smiled. Suddenly a pressure was lifted from me. I would go out there and do my best. My body has much more important uses now like carrying Ruth up the stairs to bed. Or holding Georgia's hand. Volleyball would always be my first love but since we met I had discovered even better things to love.

20

Georgia

Ruth was absolutely over the moon after the play. She gave us every detail of what happened backstage down to the costumes everyone wore. The entire car ride was non stop talking other than occasional pauses for Ashton or I to hum in acknowledgement.

We all got out of the car. I looked up and saw a very pretty starry night. Ashton had been so forgiving about my freak out and giving me space when I asked for it. I wanted to do something nice for him. He did mention he was overwhelmed with training for the charity match.

"Hey, I got a little ahead of schedule in the last couple of weeks thanks to my total isolation from society. Can I watch Ruth sometime for you? So you can practice or train or something?"

Ruth paused her third recounting of when the lion's tail fell off during the play to nod. "Yeah, Daddy! I want to hang out with Georgia!"

He laughed and nodded. "What if you came with us to

practice tomorrow? We're going to the beach to work on our stamina."

Ruth squealed at the mention of a beach. "Sounds great. I'll be there. Although I am a little exhausted tonight, can I have a rain check on the movie?"

Ruth nodded and yawned. "I'm sleepy too."

Ashton shook his head and smiled. His hand came to rest on my back as he pushed me toward my porch. "Come on then. Let's get my sleepy girls in bed."

His sweet smile killed me as I said goodnight. I congratulated Ruth one last time before heading inside and closing the door.

I kicked off my heels and headed upstairs while reaching back to unzip my dress. My earrings were the next to go as I walked to my bathroom. A makeup wipe found its way to my face and I closed my eyes as I scrubbed the day away.

I felt like a person again. The past two weeks I was nothing but a writing machine; working endlessly. I would have to thank my sister later for the wake up call. I undid my bra and went to my closet to put on the biggest t-shirt I could find.

Once in bed I fell asleep almost immediately. My eyes shut and next thing I knew my alarm was going off. I hit snooze and rolled back over. This bed was so damn comfy I never wanted to leave. Maybe being a writer was overrated. I just wanted to lay like this for the rest of my life.

And then there was a knock at my door. I sat up and checked the clock. It was only eight. Why was someone at my house? Oh shit Ashton's practice.

I jumped out of bed and threw on the closest pair of pants I could find. Running down the stairs two at a time, I made it to the door and swung it open at record speed.

Ashton looked down at my pajamas. "I realized last night I

forgot to tell you what time. I texted you but I guess you didn't see."

I nodded with my eyes closed. "Yep, just woke up. Can you give me fifteen minutes?"

He gave me a reassuring nod and Ruth walked right on in to go find Tweet. "Make yourselves comfy. I'll be quick, I promise."

Upstairs I started throwing shit frantically. We were going to the beach. Which meant a swimsuit right? I scrounged through one of my drawers to find a bikini. Then I threw on denim shorts and a t-shirt and raced to the bathroom to finish getting ready.

Ashton held up his phone screen with a time of ten minutes on the clock. The asshole timed me. I rolled my eyes and flipped him the bird behind Ruth's back. He rewarded me with a playful smile and stood up.

"What are we waiting for? Let's go to the beach."

We arrived right as the beach started to get warm. The day was nice and breezy and the sun was out and shining. We met Ashton's friends in the sand near a volleyball net.

Several eyes landed on me as we approached. "Hey, Georgia. I'm Clay, we met when you first moved in."

I smiled, thankful that he reminded me of his name. "Nice to see you again."

Ashton put his hand on my back as he turned to the rest of the guys. "Everyone, Georgia. Georgia, this is the team."

A chorus of hello's answered in response. I waved and Ruth grabbed my hand to pull me to the sidelines. Ashton took off his gym bag and set it down next to us. "I'll be right back, gotta grab your chairs."

I helped Ruth take off her shoes and we dug our toes in the

sand. "I wonder how many freckles we will get!"

"Freckles? Oh yeah, it is a very sunny day." I answered. Which reminded me.

"Do you have sunscreen on yet?"

She nodded. "Yep. Daddy put it on before we left. But he put some in the bag in case you needed it."

He really was such a dad. I looked through his gym bag to find a bottle of sunscreen and started putting it on my arms. A looming shadow hovered over me as I began rubbing in the sunscreen. I turned around to see two beach chairs and a cooler sitting behind us and Ashton watching my hand covering the rest of my arm with sunscreen.

"Want some help with that, peach?" He asked very intensely.

Well, I did need help getting my back. I turned my back to him and handed him the bottle. "Yeah, could you just get my back please?"

I lifted the hem of my t-shirt over my head and revealed my string bikini. We were at the beach and it was a hot day. There was no need to be shy or nervous but I still was when I felt his gaze trailing over my newly revealed skin. I was thankful my back was facing him so he couldn't see my blush.

Suddenly feeling the need to keep my hands busy, I cupped a hand and held it back to him. "Can I have some more so I can get my shoulders?"

I assumed he shook his head after a long pause. "I've got it. Just hold still for a minute."

Freezing cold sunscreen made goosebumps rise on my skin as he methodically started at my shoulders and worked his way down my back. We didn't speak while he worked but feeling his big hands on my body was much more tempting than I expected.

He reached the top of my shorts and stopped there. "Don't want you getting any sunburns. Your cheeks are pink enough."

His hands landed on my hips and turned me around to face him. Each of his pointer fingers had a dot of sunscreen and he swiped them over both of my cheeks. I couldn't help but chuckle at his intense expression. His eyes stayed on his work as he rubbed in the sunscreen over my cheeks, jaw, forehead, and lastly my nose.

By the time he finished I was fully mesmerized at the sight of his eyes on me. I didn't break my stare as he looked back up at me and tipped his head up. "Do you need help with anything else?"

I shook my head and grabbed the sunscreen back from him. Ruth walked back over and pointed to her newly built sandcastle. I finished up putting sunscreen on the rest of my body but left my shorts on for now.

The morning hours were spent with me and Ruth making giant sandcastles while I sneakily watched the boys warm up and start practicing. It was like a sexier version of bay watch, seeing sweaty tall men with huge muscles running and lunging for the ball. At one point they left us to go run a mile in the sand and Ashton walked over to give me a heads up. He kissed both of our heads before leaving and I had to look down at the sand castles to hide my blush.

Once they got back they started up a practice match and I quickly forgot to pretend I was making sand castles. They were really good. After Ashton's confession about being worried he wasn't performing well, I was half expecting a bunch of clumsy dads laughing and drinking while tossing a ball around. But no, these were very focused athletes.

"Georgia, look there's an ice cream cart!" My head swished

around to the direction Ruth was pointing in.

Sweat was forming in droplets on my skin and an ice cream sounded like the perfect treat for our beach day. "Do you think your dad will be mad if we eat it before lunch?"

Ruth shook her head earnestly. "Okay, let me grab my wallet." I held my hand out to her while I stood up. "What kind do you like?"

"Vanilla with sprinkles please!" I laughed.

"I wonder if anyone has made ice cream with sprinkles in the middle. Like our cupcakes."

Her head perked up and her hand rested on her belly as she thought really hard. "I don't think so. Maybe we could invent it."

"We could certainly try." We made our way up to the cart and I paid for our ice creams. Ruth held onto my shorts as we walked back to our chairs since my hands were full with both of our ice cream.

I got her all set up on the beach chair and laid a towel over her lap so she didn't spill it and get her clothes all sticky before handing her a vanilla cone with sprinkles. Her happy wiggle made me smile and I sat down next to her.

Ashton smiled over at us from where he was across the court. Ruth waved and pointed happily at her ice cream. She got a thumbs up in return before the next round started.

My goal was to do something nice for Ashton, but I think I sort of failed. A beach day, ice cream, and I get to watch him play? That's more of a treat for me than him. I started thinking of other ways to make Ashton happy while ice cream started dripping down my fingers. He had done so many thoughtful things for me without asking.

I turned to Ruth. "What's something that makes your dad

happy?"

Her focused face stopped liking her ice cream for a moment to turn to me. "Food. And my jokes." She went back to her ice cream. "Oh, and you. He smiles around you a lot."

My eyebrows shot up. "Food? What kind?"

She shrugged. "Mostly any food. He says his favorite is steak dinner. I don't really know what that is though. Uncle Nick made steak for me once and it was gross."

I laughed and leaned in so she made eye contact with me. "Do you want to help me pull off a secret mission?"

She sat up in her seat with a very colorful smile from the sprinkles. "Yes! I am good at keeping secrets."

"Good. How about we try to make a surprise dinner for your dad? He's always making food for us. It might be fun to make it for him." She nodded excitedly.

"Okay then, we should stay at the beach for a couple more hours though. It's really nice out, and I'll come up with a plan in the meantime."

Her sticky hands swept away hair from her face. "We can make steak dinner!"

I chuckled. "We will certainly try our best."

When the guys took a water break a couple hours later Ruth and I walked up to Ashton hand in hand. He smiled happily. "Hey, what have you two been up to?"

"Sandcastles! And ice cream. Georgia got me the kind with sprinkles."

Ashton laughed. "I saw. It looked great."

"We have a secret mission to go on so we need to leave now. Is that okay?" Ruth blurted out.

I winced a little. "If it's okay, Ruth and I have a secret mission that we need to go take care of. I'll turn the location on in my phone so you know where we are and I'll send updates and you can call at any second and I'll answer." He smiled and looked surprised. "And I would need to take your car. We aren't going anywhere dangerous I swear, but I do need a key to your house."

Ashton took a second to look back and forth between the two of us. Ruth and I both wore matching smiles as we waited expectantly. "Okay, but I want updates." I nodded as fast as I could. "And you'll drive safely."

"Of course, I'm a great driver." His smile widened. He leaned down to Ruth and gave her a kiss on the cheek.

He reached into his pocket for his wallet. "Not necessary! I've got it covered. Do you want me to take anything with us? And what time should we come back to pick you up?"

"You're going back to our house?" I gave him a single nod. "I'll just have Nick take me home. Don't worry about it. But be safe please. And call me if anything happens."

"I promise on my life I will! You won't regret giving me this opportunity Mr. Reid" He huffed out a laugh and gave me a look of disbelief.

He hugged Ruth again and gave her a quick talk while I gathered my stuff and grabbed my purse. Then he turned to me and said goodbye. When he turned around Ruth and I shared a big high five and huge secretive smiles.

At the grocery store I had Ruth sit in the cart and direct me to where we needed to go. We got a teensy bit distracted with chocolate and sprinkles but for the most part she did a great job. Ruth would make a great older sister, she played the part of boss a little too well.

We checked out with our food including some fancy purple potatoes, steaks, and a hamburger patty for Ruth. "Are you good at cooking?" She asked me as I pushed the cart out to the parking lot.

"Sometimes. It depends on what I'm making. But I have a Reid here to guide me so it should go pretty well." I ruffled her hair and she giggled.

We set the groceries in the trunk and I helped Ruth up into the truck and made sure she got her seatbelt on. On our way back to the house Ruth told me about how her dad tried to make purple pasta with food coloring. I nearly cried laughing when she told me the sauce turned out the worst poop brown color.

"Well our potatoes are already purple so we shouldn't have any problems there. I found a recipe on the beach for some very fancy butter braised potatoes so that should be good."

She nodded. "And he will love the flowers! He bought me some for when I did my play."

"Really?" I saw her smile in the rear view mirror. "Good! I also have some candles at my house that we can bring over. It'll be the fanciest dinner ever."

She giggled and her foot kicked my seat. We headed to my house first to grab the candles and a table cloth before unloading the rest of the groceries in the car. I snapped a picture of Ruth once we were inside to let Ashton know we made it home safely.

An hour later we were cooking with... butter. Ruth was surprisingly a very helpful sous chef. She knew where every pan or kitchen utensil was that I asked for. And she helped to taste test everything as it was finished. The purple potatoes and asparagus had gotten a very big thumbs up. Which I took as a good sign.

"Oh no, I forgot!" Ruth screeched as I was pulling some rolls out of the oven. She hopped down from her stool and raced up the stairs to her room.

"What did you forget?" A couple minutes later I was answered with the sight of Ruth in a huge floppy chef's hat and a big grin on her face.

I smiled big too. "It looks great. Now you're a real chef."

She nodded with what I assumed was supposed to be a focused look on her face. She returned to her place on the stool and kept overseeing the cooking when I placed her hamburger on the pan.

Before cooking the steak I decided it was smart to set up the table first. Hopefully if I timed everything right Ashton would walk through the door right when the steaks finished cooking so they were still nice and hot. Ruth rearranged the flowers in a glass vase while I put a white tablecloth over their kitchen table and set up some candles.

We high fived again at our progress when Ruth carefully set the vase in the middle of the table. I checked the clock again and realized Ashton should be home soon so I quickly got to cooking the steaks. Out of the corner of my eye I watched Ruth steal a pinch of bread from a roll.

I laughed and pointed to her jokingly with my tongs. "Is my sous chef *stealing* bread now?" She laughed hysterically and grabbed another pinch of bread. "Excuse me!"

My smile spread across my face and I clapped the tongs together. "No more bread for you!" Her laughs rang throughout the entire house.

I heard a knock at the wall right next to the kitchen. And then Ashton's voice spoke. I could tell he was smiling from his voice. "I know I'm supposed to be surprised, but can I come look?"

Ruth and I turned to each other in horror. "No!" We both screeched. "Not yet!" I yelled.

21

Ashton

When I opened my front door to the sound of my two girls laughing and the smell of steak, I knew to expect nothing less than an explosion in my kitchen. They told me to wait a little bit longer but there was no way I could go another second without seeing them. They left the beach two hours ago and I was dying to find out how their 'secret mission' went.

I tiptoed around the kitchen to the side door so they wouldn't hear me. My head peeked into the doorway, just wanting a quick glance but I stopped dead in my tracks. Georgia saw me first and gave me a shy smile with a blush on her face.

My eyes moved to Ruth who saw me and continued to laugh while she ran up to me. She looked up at me with a huge smile on her face and a floppy chef hat that was way too big for her head. I looked around more and saw the table was made with flowers and candles. No mess in sight.

I looked back at Georgia. She was still wearing the same t-shirt and shorts from the beach but she looked even more beautiful somehow. "I should go take a shower first. Looks like I'm underdressed for the occasion." I nodded toward the flowers. "Do I have time?"

Georgia gave me approval and shooed me back out of the kitchen. "Be quick please! The steak is almost ready!"

I gave her my best smile and turned to run upstairs. Never in my life had I been more excited to share dinner with a woman. And my daughter. I showered and made sure to scrub any remaining sand from my body.

Remembering her comment from the play, I dressed in a button down and slacks again. But this time I added a tie. I fixed my hair the best I could in a short amount of time and sprinted back downstairs.

When I reached the kitchen Ruth was standing on her stool next to the kitchen table waiting for me. "Would you like water or juice, good sir?"

I stifled my laugh at her tragic British accent. "Water is great. Thank you, jelly bean."

She giggled and walked over to Georgia who was making plates at the counter. "Can I have a glass of water?" Ruth loudly whispered.

"Sure." Georgia obnoxiously whispered back. She got a glass of water ready and carefully handed it to Ruth.

"Sit down, please." Ruth ordered and put the glass in front of me. Georgia walked over with another glass of water and a juice box. She set them down and made eye contact with that shy smile I had grown to love so much.

When Georgia returned with our plates they sat down with me and I pulled the chef hat off of Ruth's head. "Well this is quite a surprise," I said with a dopey grin on my face.

"I hope you like it. Ruth said you like steak dinner and this

166

was the best version I could come up with." Georgia put her hands on the table to stand up again. "There's more food over-"

I grabbed her hand across the table. "It's perfect. Sit down please, I want to eat dinner now."

She stared at me and sat back down slowly. She added with a smile, "The flowers are for you too."

I admired them and bit my lip to try and prevent a dumb ass smile from taking over my face again. "No one's bought me flowers before. And the candles are a nice touch."

Ruth grabbed my wrist. "And did you see the tablecloth, daddy? It's very fancy."

I felt the tablecloth in front of me. "It *is* very fancy. And are these potatoes... purple?"

The two girls shared a look and Ruth bursted out laughing while Georgia lightly laughed into her glass of water. Ruth chirped excitedly. "Yes! I told her about the pasta you made."

I hung my head in mock shame. "Let's not talk about that. We don't want to ruin this perfectly nice dinner."

Georgia asked about the rest of practice that they missed and Ruth gave me a play by play of the secret mission they went on. When Ruth was the only one of us with food left on her plate I stood up to start washing dishes.

Georgia stopped me. "No way. Sit your butt back down, this is a dinner for you. Which means you don't lift a finger."

I gave her my best dad stare. "Dinner is over though. Which means it's my turn to help."

She opened her mouth to respond when Ruth piped up. "Can we have a sleepover?"

Our stare down turned into us both staring at each other unsure of how to respond. "A sleepover?"

Ruth turned in her chair to face us. "Yeah! Georgia said she used to make forts with her sister. We can make one!"

Georgia smiled at me and nodded. So I guess that meant it was up to me to respond. "A sleepover is okay with me if it's okay with Georgia."

"We'll need lots of blankets and sheets," Georgia added while smiling up at me.

Ruth squealed and jumped up to go steal our bedding from upstairs. "Ruth, you forgot to finish your dinner!" I called.

Georgia snickered as I grabbed Ruth's plate and pushed her leftovers onto a half empty dish of asparagus. I pulled out some aluminum foil to start putting away the food we didn't get to.

When I finished I stood next to Georgia and started drying the plates she was washing. "You were supposed to sit and relax, you know. Do you want a beer?"

"Nope, I'm good." I remained where I was and kept drying the plates.

"Are you really okay with me sleeping over?" She asked nervously. I put down a plate and took the one she handed to me.

I held eye contact with her. "Of course I am. I always want you around. Are you okay with it? I can help you sneak out after she falls asleep if you want."

"You always want me around?" Her eyebrows lifted like she thought that was silly.

"I do. I thought I made that pretty clear, but it seems I must have messed up somewhere." I took the sponge from her hand to make her stop scrubbing.

Her face turned towards mine. She chose her words carefully. "Well I thought when I asked to wait until my book was over I might have messed things up."

"What made you think that?" I asked with furrowed brows. Her lips formed a tiny frown.

She stole the sponge back from me and started scrubbing again. "I think I have abandonment issues or something. Probably has to do with my mentally checked-out parents." She turned back to me. "I have no idea why I thought that. I guess I just assumed."

I looked around the kitchen. "So this was your way of apologizing- for communicating how you were feeling with me?"

She turned her eyes to the window. "Well, no. I wasn't apologizing. But I wanted to do something nice for you since you said you were stressed lately."

That made my smile return and I took the next clean plate from her. "You're pretty great. Do you know that, Georgia Mitchell?"

She scoffed and shook her head. "That's what everyone keeps telling me."

Ruth returned and we abandoned our dishes to help her build a fort out of sheets around the TV. When we were finished sheets hung above our heads and formed walls around the couch and stand that held the TV. We formed a makeshift bed out of piles of blankets and pillows on the floor in front of the couch.

I grabbed a couple of popsicles from the freezer and handed them to Georgia and Ruth before snuggling into the blanket pile next to Georgia. Ruth insisted on watching the Wizard of Oz so she could compare her play to the real deal.

As usual, my daughter fell asleep about halfway through the movie. I looked to Georgia and leaned into her ear to whisper. "I'm going to put her in bed."

She nodded and silently moved out of the way so I could scoop up Ruth and exit the pillow fort. Once upstairs I tucked her in and untied her braid so her hair freely flowed over her pillow. We would absolutely need to get her in the bath tomorrow morning. But tonight I let her sleep peacefully.

My feet carried me back downstairs to where Georgia sat, still in the pillow fort. I crouched down to not knock over any sheets and sat down next to her.

"Hey." I started.

She smiled awkwardly. "Hey."

I grabbed a pillow next to me and moved to lay down on it. "Are you sure you want to stay?" I was treating her like a deer I didn't want to scare off.

"Yeah, I am." She gave me a reassuring smile and scooched down so she could lay next to me. "I want you around all the time too."

Could she hear my heart beating? This woman was trying to give me a damn heart attack. I pushed back the hair that had fallen in her face before remembering to go at her pace. I pulled back my hand and turned so that I was laying down facing her.

She smiled and mirrored my movements. "So is this your first slumber party?" She snickered.

My eyes rolled and I smirked. "I'll have you know I've been to many slumber parties in my day."

Her teeth bit down on her lip as she held back a smile. "Well good to know I'm one of many."

I narrowed my gaze at her and she laughed. "What the hell do I have to say to get it in your pretty little head that I'm interested in you and only you?"

She laughed even harder. "I'm only messing with you."

170

I huffed and pushed a hand in my hair after rolling on my back. "Well obviously." I had totally fallen for it.

Her body moved closer to mine as she moved a few blankets out of the way. Her head rested on my shoulder and I felt her eyes on me. "Is this okay?"

I nodded slowly so I didn't scare her off. "It is."

I closed my eyes and reminded myself that we were going at her pace. I absolutely did not need to wrap my arms around her and pull her closer. I had no urges to press my face to her hair and smell the lavender shampoo I noticed on my pillow the last time she stayed.

"How have you been the last two weeks? I told you about practice and Ruth but you never told me about you."

Her head lifted from my shoulder to look at me. Her left eyebrow raised a tad like it always does when she's about to say something snarky. "You seriously don't have any guesses as to what I've been up to?"

I pushed her head back down to my shoulder and scoffed. "Other than writing. Or we can talk about writing. How has it been going? You told me you're ahead of schedule."

"Yeah, it's surprisingly good. I keep convincing myself it's complete nonsense but when I go back to read through it I am pleasantly surprised at how good it sounds. Which is rare for me." I hummed.

"And thanks for the food by the way. I would not have survived without your deliveries."

My hand rubbed at my stomach at the mention of food. I was tempted to go open the leftovers and dig into the delicious food Georgia made for me. "I know you like the tacos, what else did you like?"

"Pretty much everything. I'm not a picky eater and I was

living off of protein bars and peanut butter sandwiches so everything was great." Her hand lifted to touch the fingertips of my hand resting on my stomach. "And the notes. I really loved reading your notes."

My fingers pressed into hers as I once again intertwined our hands. She yawned and nuzzled into my chest again. "Sleepy?"

She hummed. "It's been an eventful day."

It had been. I felt exhausted too between the sun we got at the beach and the rigorous practice I did in the sand. I awkwardly shifted. As tempted as I was to sleep in a tie if it made Georgia happy, it felt a little suffocating.

My hand untangled with hers to at least untie it before sleeping. She pulled back until she was sitting up. "You're still in a tie and pants. We should change." She looked down at her own jean shorts and t-shirt.

I reached a hand out to help her up. "Come on I might have some sweats we can tie tight to fit you."

In my closet I found a pair that had a tie to hold them up on her waist and one of my favorite t-shirts. I handed them over and pointed to the bathroom. While she was in there I undid my belt and pulled down my slacks. I was hanging them back up when she exited the bathroom.

Her eyes trailed down my body to my legs while I did the same to her. She walked up to me confidently with those sleepy eyes. Hands raised to my undone tie and she pulled it off to hand to me. Her hands then trailed down to start unbuttoning my shirt for me.

I watched her face intently. Trying to memorize everything about this moment and never forget it. She reached the bottom button and stood still. Her lips tilted up in a smile as she looked up at me. "I absolutely adore your tattoos," she said as her hand traced over them.

My hand reached up to hold her wrist. I had patience, and I would be patient for Georgia. But if she started teasing me there was no way I would be able to hold back. She leaned up and pulled her wrist back to wrap her arms around my shoulders.

Her face hovered in front of mine as I looked over her sweet expression. She looked blissfully happy with her mouth curved in a soft smile. "I'm going to kiss you now, Ashton. And I promise I won't run after."

My breathing hitched and I let her lips press softly against mine. She started out slow, testing me. When she felt my lips start to move against hers she pulled me even closer by my neck and kissed me harder. She let out a soft moan as my hand moved to cradle the back of her head.

She was everything, this was everything. I would never be able to let her go. I needed her more than I needed air. But I promised to go at her pace.

I pulled back slightly and we breathed slowly with our mouths almost touching. I pushed my forehead to hers and whispered, "We should go to bed."

Even I cringed at the words and Georgia frowned. My hand came up to hold her chin and I let my inner thoughts drive my actions when I placed my thumb on her bottom lip and pulled it down.

She kissed my thumb and said, "Why? Are you tired?"

I sighed, "I'm wide fucking awake now. You just kissed me. But we talked about this and you're half asleep so we should go to bed."

Her teeth bit at my thumb now playfully, "I thought we were going at my pace. I want you now."

I shut my eyes to focus. She really wasn't making this easy. My dick felt harder than it ever had in my entire damn life.

Regretfully I spoke, "Your eyelids are half closed, baby. When we do this you're going to remember every second of it. I want you wide awake, aware, and excited." I gave her a quick peck on the nose. "Now stop teasing me and let's get back to our fort."

She nodded sleepily and stared at me with a dreamy look on her face. Maybe she did think this was all a dream. I finished pulling the unbuttoned shirt off of my shoulders. After hesitating, I figured it would be best to put on a t-shirt.

We headed back downstairs and laid down in the piles of blankets and pillows. Her head found its way back to my shoulder and I wrapped my arm around her back this time. I waited until her breath evened and slowed down before letting myself fall asleep.

22

Georgia

Something cold and wet tickled my foot and I was brought back to consciousness. Ashton's warm body surrounded me but I pulled back to look at what was touching my feet. I blinked and wiggled my toes as I felt it on my big toe next.

I fully sat up to look down at Ruth. My arm raised to rub the sleep out of my eyes. "What are you doing?"

She sneakily laughed and held up a blue marker. "I'm making faces on your toes." She whispered.

This had to go in my top ten for weirdest ways to wake up. I looked back at Ashton to see he was still dead asleep and blushed. His hair was pointing in every direction and he even had a little bit of drool on the pillow. How cute.

Ruth moved to Ashton's toes next since mine were pulled back beneath the blankets. Still half asleep, I had no idea what I was supposed to do in this situation. So I just laid back down on Ashton's chest and let her have at it.

Minutes later Ashton jerked out of sleep and gently pulled

his arm out from under me. He sat up and whisper-yelled, "What the hell are you doing Ruth?"

She laughed and pointed at his toes. I decided it was best to stop pretending to sleep and sat up too. He looked over at me and his blush covered his entire face including his ears. I wasn't sure if he was blushing over the fact that Ruth had caught us cuddling or not.

"Good morning," he whispered to me. I smiled and murmured the greeting back. He turned back to Ruth. "Good morning, troublemaker. Come here, my little toe artist."

His hands slid under her armpits as he lifted her up to sit her back down with us in the blanket pile. She found her way to sit in the middle of us and recapped her marker. Her smile took up nearly her entire face.

"Can we go to Uncle Nick's for breakfast?" Ashton scrubbed a hand over his face before looking his daughter in the eyes.

"Yes, but you need a bath. Like yesterday kid. Let's go get you ready." He stood up and then turned back to me and his blush returned.

He paused to think. "Will you come to breakfast with us please?"

I rose to my own two feet and tried to remember where I put my clothes last night. "Sure, I should go shower and get dressed too though."

He patted Ruth on the back and leaned down to her. "Why don't you go pick out your clothes for me?"

She nodded and raced up the stairs. Once we were alone he turned back to me. He murmured, "I'm sorry if I was too touchy last night. Will you please come to breakfast with us?"

So that's what he was so blushy over. "If I remember correctly I was the one who felt you up first." I walked up and rubbed at the drool on his chin with my thumb. I flashed him a pleased smile. "I'll be back in about thirty minutes. That okay?"

He nodded and stared at me before deciding to pull me into his chest in a hug. "Don't take too long please." His voice sounded low and desperate. Ashton Reid was needy in the morning.

"I'll be right back," I promised.

I left Ashton's clothes on as I made a -sort of- walk of shame back to my house. My shower was turned to the hottest setting and I scrubbed everything as fast as I could. After drying my hair and changing into my own clothes I checked my phone before heading back over to my neighbor's house.

"Daddy, Georgia is coming to Uncle Nick's right?" I heard Ruth ask as I was opening the door.

"She said she would, she just had to go home and take her own bath first." Ruth nodded and turned in her seat to see me when I knocked on the wall next to the light switch.

Both Reid's gave me bright smiles as I walked into the living room. Ruth was sitting in front of the couch between his legs and Ashton was crouched over braiding her hair into two cute little pigtails.

"You can braid?" The words came out of my mouth before I could even process them.

He gave me a dirty look. "Of course I can, Mitchell. I'm a dad."

I moved to sit down on the couch next to them as I watched them work. Ruth made sure to let me know he was good at it too. "Daddy, you should braid Georgia's hair too."

He shot me a questioning look. "If you want to, I wouldn't mind. I only had time to dry it."

I ran a hand through my long hair before glancing back at him. He finished up with Ruth and pulled the end of one of her pigtails before asking her to get up. He turned his body so it was facing mine and spun his finger in a circle. "Turn around please."

"I'll go grab another hair tie!" Ruth exclaimed.

My body turned a little to look at him. "Can I have only one braid please?"

He laughed under his breath. "Only because you asked nicely."

It took less than five minutes for Ashton to braid my hair. His fingers brushed my neck as he let me know he was finished. My body shivered and I went to look in the mirror. He actually did a good job. I adjusted it to how I wanted and loosened it up a bit before turning back to them. "Ready to go?"

We all arrived at Reid's Diner before the breakfast rush. Nick looked surprised to see us walk in together and had us sit down at the bar top.

"Hey Ruthie, good morning." He turned to me next. "Good morning, Georgia. Nice to see you again."

I smiled and returned the greeting. "Yeah, good morning brother. Nice to see you too." Ashton said to himself and Ruth laughed.

I was beginning to notice she really enjoyed seeing her dad and uncle argue. I had blueberry pancakes in front of me faster than I could blink. Ashton had eggs and bacon and Ruth's took a little longer because hers was 'special'. Breakfast was mostly silent while we all wolfed down our food.

Ruth broke the silence first. "Do I have swim today?"

Ashton's head shook. "Nope, that's tomorrow."

Nick walked back from helping a customer. "What are you

178

three up to today?"

"Just breakfast for now. I promised Stone we could weight train together later though." Ashton paused from devouring his food to take a gulp of orange juice.

"Georgia, do you play any sports? I play soccer now." Ruth asked.

I swallowed a bite of pancake. "I was a mean mini golf player back in my day. Didn't quite make it to the Olympics though." I winked at Ashton.

He snorted and smiled into his food. "Mini golf? Can we try it daddy?"

He gave me a side eye as if that was my question to answer. "Does Rosewood have a mini golf course?"

Nick answered next. "Yeah, there's one right up the street. Over on Mayfield."

Ashton and I exchanged a glance. "Mini golf only takes about thirty minutes. I'm sure I can whoop your butts and be back at home to write in no time."

His eyebrows raised at the challenge. "You're on. Let's see what the great Georgia Mitchell can do with a putt putt club."

I almost choked on my water before finishing the rest of my pancakes as fast as possible. Ruth and Ashton ate fast. I needed to pick up the pace if I wanted to keep up.

We made it to the mini golf course right when they opened at ten. The attendant looked exhausted and about ready to quit. Ashton paid and carried our clubs for us while Ruth and I picked out which color ball we wanted.

The game started out fair. We each took turns and Ash kept track of our scores on his phone. Ruth needed help to get the hang of it so we took turns helping her out. But then on the third hole I had a great idea.

Ashton was counting up the scores on his phone to see where we were all at while Ruth and I waited for him. I waved to Ruth behind his back. Then I made sure to look up at the sky and 'accidentally' knock his red ball into a ditch of sand.

Little girl giggles interrupted the early morning quiet. Ashton snapped up from his phone and looked around for what she was laughing at. His suspicious gaze looked to my face and then down to find his ball now in sand.

"How did that happen?" He asked. His tone was trying to be serious but the smile on his face clearly gave him away.

I pretended to be interested in my fingernails. "What are you talking about?"

He stalked over to hit his ball out of the sand. "I see how you play now, peach. Watch your back." He whispered.

I bit my lip and we continued on. The next hole Ruth put her foot out in front of his ball that was headed directly for the hole. I covered my mouth as Ashton turned to look pointedly at me. "Do you see what you've started?"

I laughed behind my hand and felt a little guilty. On my next putt Ashton slammed his club down right in front of the hole and I could only laugh. "Daddy! That is *cheating!*"

He stared at his own daughter with his mouth hanging open. The blatant favoritism made my heart squeeze. But I took the shot anyway and added another point to my score. We played the cheating game for several more rounds. At one point Ashton bumped into Ruth's elbow as she was putting.

The last hole had a huge shark that you putt into its mouth and it 'ate' your ball. I went first and Ashton literally moved to stand in front of me. I looked up and waited but his face told me he was not going to move. So I tried to hit the ball anyway.

It bounced off of his shoe and rolled backwards. "That's

one."

I rolled my eyes and tried again. His foot kicked out in front of the ball again. "Two."

Ruth stomped over and playfully yelled. "Daddy! Move!"

She tried to climb up his leg to distract him while I continued putting the ball.

We were all exhausted and breathless from laughing by the time he counted. "Twenty two."

I pretended to lay down my club in defeat. Ashton held on to the monkey trying to climb him and moved to sit down and catch his breath. Within seconds I used the flat club to knock my ball into the very easy shark tunnel in one hit.

"Well played." He huffed out. Ruth plopped down next to him.

We all sat for a moment catching our breath before Ashton took his turn. I held Ruth's hand to let him have a shot without having to deal with our cheating. Then we both helped Ruth lineup her shot and she got it in only two hits.

After returning the clubs back to the attendant Ashton counted up all of our scores from his phone as we walked to the parking lot. I rolled my eyes as he had Ruth drumroll for the final results.

He cleared his throat before speaking. "And in first place we have... Ashton Reid! In a major upset as he defeats the long time champion Georgia Mitchelllll." He said in his best announcer voice.

On the way home Ruth asked to join a club for mini golf and Ashton promised to check if there was one in Rosewood. She filled the silence as usual while we filled her pauses with sounds of acknowledgement and threw in a few questions every now and then. Ashton pulled in his driveway.

I mentally started preparing for getting back into writing mode as we all piled out of the truck. I bent down to hug Ruth and say goodbye. She squeezed me extra tight and I promised to see her again soon. Then Ashton hugged me too and kissed the top of my head.

"Good luck writing, peach. We're right next door." I smiled and headed back to my house.

23

Ashton

I was putting Ruth to bed that night when she said exactly how I'd been feeling for the last three weeks. "I wish Georgia could stay the night again."

"You do?" I sat down and sighed. I'd been meaning to have this conversation with her but wasn't sure exactly how to go about it.

She nodded and pulled the covers up to her chin. "I like having Georgia around too, kid. So if Georgia came around more that would make you happy?"

She smiled and nodded again. The kid wasn't giving me a lot to work with. "How would you feel if I hung out with Georgia too sometimes? You know how you get alone time with her?"

Her tiny face stilled for a moment before responding. "Like a date?"

I wasn't in the habit of lying to my daughter so I nodded. "I knew it would work!" She exclaimed.

"What would work?" My brow furrowed.

She sat up out of bed excitedly. "The beach! We went to the

beach with lots of sun and now Georgia thinks you're pretty and she'll go on a date with you."

I laughed and pinched her cheek. "Yeah, yeah, I guess you were right after all. She hasn't said yes yet. I wanted to ask you first. How would that make you feel if Georgia and I went on a date?"

Her smile kicked in full time as she beamed up at me. "Happy! Duh."

I pretended to flick her forehead and rolled my eyes. "Alright, brat. Lay back down." I smiled and leaned down to kiss where I flicked her. "I love you. More than anything in the whole world."

"I love you too, daddy." She stretched her neck to kiss my cheek.

The next week I went into crunch time training for the charity match. I was running miles a day while Ruth was at her various activities. And when she wasn't she came to the gym with me while I continued practicing either on my own or with anyone who was free that day.

Georgia came over a few times with breakfast for us. I was extra thankful for those mornings because figuring out how to throw together a meal was one less thing I needed to worry about. As if on cue from my thoughts about her, my doorbell rang and Georgia entered my home.

She had a box of what I assumed were baked goods in one hand and a book in the other. "Good morning!" She seemed happy lately.

"Good morning, peach." I wrapped an arm around her and looked down at the box. "What do you have for us?"

"I know you're eating healthy and all before the match but I read carbs were important for when you're training. So I got you a blueberry muffin. I didn't make them, they're from the next town over. I passed by when I was picking this up." She lifted the book.

The Wizard of Oz. I smiled and took the box from her hand and leaned in for a sneaky kiss on the cheek.

Lately everything seemed so easy with Georgia. We were on the same page finally, which was- . That we cared about each other? That we wanted to see each other more? I knew that I wanted a full blown serious relationship. I'm not sure when that happened but there was no doubt in my mind Georgia was the only one I would ever want.

But she had never explicitly said that's what she wanted. We were going at her pace so it felt wrong to ask the cliche 'what are we?'. Before I could spiral into full blown panic mode I brought the box of baked goods to the kitchen.

"Where's Ruth?" Georgia asked. She was dressed in her classic soft t-shirt and shorts ensemble. She was practically glowing with happiness.

"Getting dressed upstairs. Are you still coming to the charity match?" She nodded.

"Of course, it's a week from today right?" I nodded back at her and picked a muffin out of the box before sitting down.

She sat down across from me. "Are you still nervous?"

I sighed. "A little. The pressure is getting to me a bit."

She frowned. "Would it help if I took Ruth for a day? Or even a half day?"

"Your book is due in a few days isn't it? I've got it covered. We'll be just fine, just have to get through this week of practice." I ran a hand through my hair.

She smiled shyly. "Actually, I finished it today. The final rough draft at least. I'm going to take three more days to edit it and triple check that it's good but it's all written down now. I feel like I just finished climbing Mount Everest."

"You finished it?" I said incredulously. "That's great. Why didn't you tell me?"

"I only finished last night!" She beamed. "I'm going to get a hot chocolate from that coffee shop near the diner to celebrate."

Ruth stepped into the kitchen with impeccable timing. "Hot chocolate! Can I come?"

I looked to Georgia. She nodded with the same shy smile. "Georgia finished her book. I say we should go buy her a hot chocolate. What do you think, Ruth?"

"Definitely! Are those muffins?" Her tiny five-year old hands reach for the box from the bakery.

Georgia explained. "They are. I got you blueberry and chocolate chip, so you can decide which you want. I also picked this up." She held up the Wizard of Oz book like a trophy.

Ruth squinted at it. "What is it?"

Georgia's laugh lit up her face. "Right, I forgot you can't read yet. It's the Wizard of Oz!"

That made Ruth smile. She bit into a blueberry muffin and started flipping through the pages of the book as if she was suddenly capable of reading full on chapter books. We each sat at the table eating our muffins before heading to my truck.

I drove us to the coffee shop and basked in the glow of a happy Georgia. Once we walked through the door an older woman greeted us. "Welcome in! What can I get for you three?"

"Two hot chocolates and a black coffee please." I would need the caffeine for practice later. The woman typed in numbers at the register until a total popped up. I got out my card and paid for it.

"Thanks, Ash." Georgia whispered. Her giving me a nickname was enough to make me weak in the knees. I smiled over my shoulder at her and shoved my card back in my wallet.

The woman helping us spoke up. "Whipped cream on the hot chocolates?"

Georgia and Ruth made eye contact before Ruth gave a quick nod. Georgia answered for her. "Yes, please."

We moved to sit at a table near the pick up counter while our drinks were made. I put my ankle against hers under the table. My hand was itching to hold hers but I wasn't sure if she was ready for that yet. At least I'd had a conversation with Ruth and knew for sure where she stood.

Now I just had to get the other woman in my life on board and we would be golden.

"Here you go!" The woman called out to us. I stood up to grab the drink tray. "You have a beautiful family by the way, son. Never take that for granted."

I blinked before smiling. "I won't. Thank you very much ma'am."

Georgia walked up next to me. "Do you want help carrying those?" She looked down at the tray with our drinks.

"Now is this your wife?" The older woman asked me pointedly. Shit. I wasn't expecting Georgia to overhear this pretend family situation.

She looked at me confused for a second before turning to the woman. Before she could speak I spoke for her. "Not yet."

Georgia's eyes widened comically. She relaxed her face into a smile and put her hand on my arm. I was not expecting her to play along but now that she was I would never recover.

"Well, you better put a ring on that finger soon. It looks like she already has a few of her own to choose from." She pointed at Georgia's hand that was covered in rings.

My girl only laughed and twisted at one, her arm now interlocked with mine. "He will soon. I'm sure of it."

Her eyes met mine and I held her stare. I forgot to breathe before Ruth broke our trance. "Are we drinking them here? I thought we were going back home."

I grabbed the tray again and we thanked the woman before exiting her coffee shop. Ruth skipped back to the car happily while Georgia and I walked arm in arm. She smiled up at me playfully and squeezed my arm. "I didn't know you wanted to play house with me."

I didn't even hesitate to roll my eyes. "I'll play house with you any time Mrs. Reid."

Her cheeks were red faster than I could blink. I opened the car door for her before helping Ruth into her seat in the back. Georgia held onto the drink tray while I drove and sipped on her hot chocolate in silence.

I pulled my truck in the driveway. "Careful, daddy. Don't run into the house."

Georgia shot me an amused glance. "I won't run into the house. It happened one time."

That brought out a full blown smile. We got out of the car and Georgia passed us our drinks. "Thank you very much for the hot chocolate."

I raised my coffee. "To writing books."

She slowly tapped her cup to mine before bending down to tap it to Ruth's too. "I was serious about my offer earlier. Just let me know what day works best for you. I'll be editing for the next three days but I'm free anytime after.

She walked backwards towards her house. "I'll remember

that. Go finish your best seller."

Ruth yelled. "Bye!"

Georgia waved to both of us and headed back inside her house. I took another sip of my coffee before wincing and following Ruth into ours.

24

Georgia

After I finished editing and submitting my final draft to my client, I waited for Ashton to reach out. He called on the day it was due to congratulate me but said he had to go soon after because he was picking Ruth up from swim practice. I opened my door the next morning to a warm hot chocolate which was nice.

Now that my book wasn't taking over my thoughts constantly most of my attention was focused on Ashton and Ruth. He pretended to want to marry me the last time we were together, but we hadn't ever spoken about what we actually wanted. Hopefully tonight we could have a moment alone together after his match to talk about it.

I really wanted him. More than anything I had ever wanted in my entire life. Ashton Reid had found his way into my heart and I wanted nothing more than for him to keep it and hold onto it for safekeeping. I wondered if Ruth was one of the reasons he might be hesitant. She had quickly become one of my best friends in my time here. But I understood that she might be wary of her dad being in a new relationship.

My shower was hot as usual and steam covered the entire mirror when I stepped out of it. "Georgia?"

I whipped around to see Ashton standing in my room. I still had nothing but a towel on and he stood frozen like a deer in headlights. "Um. Did you need something?"

His mouth opened and closed a few times. He lifted his arm to show me he was holding something in his hand. "My jersey."

I looked at his face to try and decipher what the hell he was trying to say. "My jersey. I thought you might want to wear it. You know, to the match."

"Oh, right. Yeah I would love to." I reached for it and he handed it over. His eyes devoured every inch of my uncovered skin.

"Right, well I should probably get back. Come over when you're ready." He sounded like he was in some kind of trance. I nodded and he turned his head before heading out of my bedroom and leaving my house.

I didn't have Ashton breaking in my house to spy on me in the shower on my bingo list for today but it wasn't an unwelcome event. I really needed to talk to him. I needed to tell him my feelings before my nerves got the best of me.

I put on a bra and underwear before slipping the jersey over my head. The jersey was big and seeing Reid spelled out on my back made warmth bloom in my stomach. Now I understand why men did this. It was like claiming their territory by literally having their name written on women's backs.

While it was very caveman-like, I hoped Ashton wanted to claim me for good. And for the right reasons. I trusted him with my heart and now with my back too. I finished getting dressed and slipped on sneakers before heading out the door to walk over to Ashton's house.

Nick was there when I arrived. Ruth ran up to say hi and I waved to both Ashton and Nick. Ashton looked a little mortified, I'm guessing because he walked in on me in the shower. But what exactly was he expecting? We piled in Nick's car and headed to the charity match.

Ruth showed off her hair that had streaks spray painted in the team's colors of red and blue. Then she sat up and reached toward her dad. "Did you bring the bracelet?"

Ashton nodded and reached in his bag to fish something out. He handed it over to Ruth who passed it over to me. "It's a blue bracelet. Like the one I had when we helped you move. Daddy helped me make it so now we can match!"

She raised her tiny arm to show me the beaded bracelet on her wrist. My heart felt tight as I pulled it on my own wrist and held it up to hers. "I love it. Thank you, Ruth."

Her smile was blinding and she bumped her wrist to mine.

The charity match was held in a city an hour outside of Rosewood. When we exited the car Ashton pulled me over to talk while Nick stayed with Ruth by the car. "There are going to be a lot of people here so I need you to hold her hand in the crowds."

I nodded. "I promise I'll take good care of her. We're going to have a great time. And you're going to do great." I poked his chest.

He nodded to himself. "Right. Just pre-game nerves." He smiled. "Thank you for coming. I feel much better knowing I've got you to cheer for me in the crowd."

I gave him my best smirk. "Always, Reid. Your name is even written across my back in case you forget it. Now go win a game so we can celebrate after."

His laugh was playful. "Just so you're prepared. I don't celebrate wins by drinking hot chocolate, princess."

"Good to know. I'll keep that in mind." I pushed his chest lightly. "Now go win so you can show me how you celebrate."

He flashed me one last winning smile before returning to Ruth and giving her a kiss. Nick said goodbye and I wished them both luck before taking Ruth's hand and heading inside. Since this was a charity match it was sort of a free for all in terms of seating. Luckily we arrived early so we managed to find seats towards the front.

"Reese is coming too. Do you think she's here already?" I asked Ruth.

She shook her head. "I don't know. Maybe you can call her."

I decided to text her instead and set my purse down in a chair next to us in case she needed a seat. The giant arena where the match was being held filled up quickly. I spotted Reese's curly head of hair walking through the entrance and stood to wave her down.

She didn't see me but the giant volleyball player trailing close behind her did. Ryan leaned down to talk in Reese's ear and pointed in our direction. They headed towards us and I sat down on the other side of Ruth so she could sit between Reese and I with Ryan on the other end.

Reese was carrying a handful of posters. "Hey! You guys made it!"

I smiled at her and held out a hand to hold the posters for her while she sat down. "What's all of this?"

"My kids made them, turns out the youth of Rosewood idolize Reid and Summers. They couldn't come so they wanted to show their support somehow." She helped me set them down against the barrier in front of us.

Reese turned to lean down in front of Ruth. "Are you so excited to watch your dad play?"

She nodded shyly and reached for my hand. Crowds weren't exactly my idea of fun either so I understood why she might not feel super social with all of the noise going on around us.

I leaned back to greet Ryan. "Hey, I didn't know you were coming!"

He leaned his arm over the back of Reese's seat. "I played with half of these oldies back in high school. If I didn't come I would never hear the end of it."

I laughed and tuned back in to Reese showing Ruth all of the posters her kids made. She let Ruth pick one out to hold up for her dad. It was hard to talk as the gym filled up. Everyone seemed to be over the moon excited about the match that was starting up right below us.

As the players started walking out on the court I squeezed Ruth's hand and leaned down to her level. "Do you see your dad? He's right over there."

She smiled and followed my finger. "And that's Uncle Nick!" She pointed out her uncle who was still in a black t-shirt.

"Is Uncle Nick not playing? Where's his jersey?" I asked.

She leaned up and yelled in my ear. "He's the coach!"

I nodded surprised. Well I guess they did need a coach and Ashton's brother seemed like the bossy type. A lot like my sister now that I thought about it.

The game finally started and I found myself on the edge of my seat watching Ashton play. Neither team had come unprepared. It seemed like each round they went back and forth with the points.

This was my first sports game I had seen live since high school. I wasn't expecting to be so entranced but I was. Ashton

194

playing made my heart race with adrenaline as if I was playing in the game myself. Each time he served my hands clenched into fists. I gasped as he dove for a ball and missed as it hit the ground.

Who knew I could be a volleyball fan? We won the first round and I screamed with everyone else in the crowd. All four of us stood up out of our seats to hold the signs and I reached over to help Ruth hold hers up. We both waved as Ashton looked up into the stands and gave us my favorite smile.

The game went by fast and everytime we scored a major point I screamed my head off. It was fun to act like a complete caveman I was realizing. Ruth was having fun screaming too. We beamed at each other when I checked in halfway through the match that she was still having a good time.

We were tied and the next point would decide if the Rose-wood team would win it all or they would keep playing. Ryan leaned over and yelled. "They have to win this now if they want to take it home."

I turned back to the game and squeezed Ruth's hand hard. They absolutely had to win. I knew how hard Ashton worked to get here and he deserved to win this more than anything. Ruth squeezed my hand back as we watched the other team fumble for the ball to get it over the net. And... it hit the ground. We won!

All of the Rosewood boys on the court jumped on each other in a giant group hug. Reese hugged me and trapped Ruth between us while we were all standing and screaming our heads off. Ryan had a huge smile on his face and high fived Ruth.

The excitement that ran through my veins was crazy. I felt more pumped than when I finished my book. And I absolutely could not wait to see Ashton.

We sat back down while everyone else started piling out of the gym. Ryan and Reese started asking Ruth about what she thought of her dad playing. I sat quietly and processed all of my emotions and my head felt like it was buzzing.

Once the gym was mostly empty we headed down to the entrance to find Ashton and the others. I spotted his blonde head in between the other tall players and waved. He weaved through everyone and practically sprinted over to us with a huge smile on his face.

He lifted Ruth into the air and spun her around before holding her in one arm and grabbing me into a hug with his other. "You won, daddy!"

His smile was so bright it hurt. "That was amazing! Best volleyball playing I've ever seen in my life."

He squeezed us harder and kissed Ruth's cheek. "That's all thanks to my fans. Couldn't have done it without you two."

I rolled my eyes at the word fans but kept my smile. He pulled me back into my own hug while Ruth ran to get her hug from Nick. "You really were great."

"Thanks, peach. Are you ready to celebrate now?" I snickered. His smile told me he was planning something that I should be hesitant about. What exactly was he planning to do with a five year old tagging along?

Ryan slapped him on the back. "Nice job, Reid. You weren't so bad after all."

"Shut it Summers. You wish you could play like me." The two exchanged a dorky man handshake.

Reese piped up, "I have to be at school for some dumb teacher planning day tomorrow morning. Do you want me to take Ruth home while you two go out and celebrate?"

Well there goes the five year old theory. Ashton looked to me and then back at Reese. "She'll have to go to bed soon. I'm not sure if she would be okay with doing bedtime without me."

Reese nodded. "We could all go back to yours then. You can put her to bed and I'll sleep on the couch while you all go out."

Ashton's eyebrows furrowed. "I'll ask her." He turned to me. "Is that alright with you?"

I looked at Reese. "I can stay with her if you want to go out. I'm not big on bars."

Ashton and Reese both shook their heads at the same time. "No way, peach. You've got to go out and meet your new town. Your book is finished so it's time to put yourself out there. I'll go ask Ruth."

Ashton left us to talk to Nick and Ruth. Reese looked at me with a smile. "You are so going so don't even think of trying to get out of it. You haven't experienced life until you've been to a bar after a volleyball game at Rosewood."

I nodded my head. I doubted I would find it as fun as she said but I also hadn't expected to like the volleyball game.

25

Ashton

Once we got approval from Ruth to go ahead with the plan we all headed back to my house. After the rush from winning I felt on top of the world. And now I was going to spend the night with Georgia at my side celebrating my win. Nothing could beat this.

At home I took Ruth upstairs while the others waited in my living room. We got her in pajamas and brushed her teeth before I sat her down to brush out her hair. "I was so happy to watch you play, daddy."

"So was I, pumpkin. I'm glad you liked it." She nodded and held on tight to her teddy bear while I finished her hair.

"Are you sure you're okay staying with Reese while I go out for a few hours?"

She smiled. "Georgia is going. Is this your date?"

I laughed and pinched her cheek. "Not yet. But I'm thinking about asking her tonight."

She scooched back to lay down on her pillow. "Make sure you say please, daddy."

"I will. I promise." I kissed her head and told her goodnight one more time. "If you change your mind and want me to come home for any reason, just tell Reesey okay?"

She hugged her teddy bear to her chest and nodded. I flicked off the lights and left the door cracked open before heading downstairs. Everyone turned to me and I grabbed a jacket since it would probably be cold. I would be fine but Georgia would probably want it later.

"I promise I will call if I so much as hear a peep." Reese held up three fingers like a girl scout.

I laughed and gave her a side hug. "I really appreciate you watching her. I told her to ask you if she gets scared or something and wants me to come home."

I turned to Georgia. "You ready to celebrate?"

Her shy smile returned once again. Which made me smile in full force. Little did she know she would meet most of the people in town our age tonight at the packed bar. There was no chance in hell I was leaving her side though, so she had nothing to worry about.

"Ready." She responded. We headed out and Ryan joined Nick in his car this time. Georgia and I piled in the truck in case I needed to go home to Ruth.

I talked about the match today while Georgia sat quietly. We were alone in the truck so I grabbed her hand and held it until we got to the bar. Once inside her eyes widened a little at the crowd.

"Just stick by me, okay?" She nodded. "It'll be fun. Everyone will have seen the match so we're all just here to have a good time."

With Georgia's habit of hiding when she got stressed, I wouldn't have been surprised if she had never been to a packed bar like this. I walked up to the bar and ordered two beers for us. Seconds later a man I recognized from the crowd today yelled. "Reid!"

I smiled as he walked over and slapped me on the shoulder. "Nice job today, man." He waved over the bartender. "Hey, two shots for me and the man of the hour over here."

I shot a look over to Georgia and she seemed happy. I downed the shot with the stranger before grabbing our beers and dragging us over to a table where some of my teammates and Ryan sat.

Over the next hour Georgia opened up a little and joined the conversation with everyone. Seeing that she warmed up to them, the guys started hounding her with questions about what the hell she saw in me. She blushed and I saved her from having to answer every time. As if on a timer, every fifteen minutes another person would buy our table a shot.

I started to feel tipsy around the fifth shot and realized I haven't gotten drunk in years. I probably should have paced myself. But it was too late for that now. I looked over at Georgia through hazy eyes and didn't stop myself from staring at her.

She leaned in. "You okay?"

I smiled dreamily and nodded. She laughed at my reaction. "Maybe you should switch to water." She pushed my beer away.

"Can we go home now?" I asked. I just wanted to be alone with her and stare at her pretty face. And I wanted to check on my daughter.

She nodded and pushed my arm to slide out of the booth. "I'm headed home, gentlemen." I saluted. "Stay safe and have fun."

Ryan stood up with Georgia. "Do you want help getting him

home?"

I glared at him and waved him off. I wasn't *that* drunk. Georgia shrugged and leaned down to slip my arm over her shoulders. "No, he seems pretty stable. I've got it. Thanks, though Ryan."

She waved goodbye to everyone else and we walked to the exit together. Once in the parking lot I removed my arm from her shoulders and grabbed my keys out of my pocket. I looked down trying to find the right one when I realized.

"Oh, I should call us an Uber." She shook her head and held out her hand.

I stared at it until she said. "Hand over the keys, Reid. I've only had half of a beer and I promise not to run into the house."

I put them in her open palm and she guided me to the passenger side. "Hey, I should be opening the door for you."

She laughed. "Maybe when you're not so wobbly. Keep your arms out of the door." She said before shutting it gently.

The drive home was quiet and I took the opportunity to stare at her face without interruption. She looked over and caught me a few times but it didn't deter me. I wanted to kiss those pretty pink lips so badly.

She helped me out of the car and up the stairs of my porch. I stumbled a little but she caught me and I got inside without any injuries. "I wouldn't think anyone so big could be a lightweight."

I furrowed my eyebrow at her. "I'm not a lightweight. I just haven't gotten drunk in a while."

She smiled and put her finger to the pout on my lips. "Do you want to go tell Ruth goodnight?"

I nodded and she walked around the couch to wake up a sleeping Reese. I left them as I headed up the stairs to go kiss my baby girl goodnight. She was deep asleep when I found her so I kissed her forehead and tucked her in before going back downstairs.

Reese was standing up now and grabbing her things. "There he is. Heard you got a little too celebratory."

I rolled my eyes. "I'm just fine. Are you okay to drive home?"

She laughed and exchanged a look with Georgia. "I'm good." She walked up and lightly tapped me on the cheek. "You go easy on her okay? She's been good to you."

I had no clue what that meant but I nodded and said goodbye anyway. Once Georgia saw she got to her car safely she shut the front door and came to sit next to me on the couch with a bottle of water. "Drink this, please."

I grabbed the bottle and put it up to my lips. I tilted it up a little too fast and water spilled down my chin onto my shirt. She snickered at me while I used my damp shirt to wipe off my chin. I smiled at her laugh and stared at her again.

Her eyes were the most beautiful thing I had ever seen. And Ruth was right, she had cute little freckles now dotting across her nose and up her cheeks. Her lips were curved into a smile as she looked back at me.

"I'm so in love with you." I said. I wanted to bottle up her smile and put it in my pocket all day every day so I could take a peek whenever I wanted. I looked up from her lips to see her eyes had widened.

Did I say something? She looked freaked out. I reached a hand out to her face and frowned. "What's wrong?"

She held my wrist and returned it back to my lap. Oh, I definitely fucked up. "Do you need help getting to bed? You probably need some sleep. It's been a long day and you had a lot to drink."

I frowned and stared at her some more. What was she thinking? Where did that cute confused face come from? I nodded and let her help me up. "Did I say something stupid? Why are you upset?"

She sighed. "Not upset, just tired is all. Let's get you to bed, we can talk more tomorrow."

She helped me upstairs and set me down on my bed. "Hand me your keys so I can lock the house behind me."

I grabbed the keys that were digging into my leg through my pocket. "You're not staying?"

She offered me a small smile. "Not tonight. You need to rest, but if you want we can talk tomorrow. Okay?" Her words were robotic almost.

I nodded even though I really wanted her to stay. I would see her tomorrow and that was good enough for now. She helped me turn over onto my side and pulled out my phone from my pocket too and set it on the bedside table.

"Goodnight, Ashton."

My hand pushed back my hair and I lifted my face to see her more clearly. "Goodnight, peach. Will you text me that you got home safe?"

She laughed lightly. "I will."

26

Georgia

He's in love with me. Well at least his drunk brain was. And I had no idea what to do with that. Why would he only say that while drunk? We were having such a good day and by the time he had his third shot I decided to hold off the conversation about what we were for another day. But then he went and did that.

I had read briefly before about people confessing their feelings while drunk and it was almost never a good sign. After I got home from Ashton's house I stayed up for hours pouring over both credible and non credible threads online about what it meant if a man confessed to you while drunk. The signs were not looking great.

After I had read nearly everything on the internet about the subject I shut down my laptop. It was practically almost sunrise so I put on a trashy romcom and laid on my couch. The movie finished around seven and I realized Ruth would probably be waking up soon.

I was doing no good wallowing on my couch so I went to

pick up breakfast from a drive thru coffee place. I settled on a breakfast sandwich for Ashton and some pancakes for Ruth. Thankfully I stole Ashton's keys from him yesterday so getting inside wasn't a problem. The plan was to sneak inside and leave the food on the kitchen table.

But then Ruth was sitting on the couch when I walked in. "Is that breakfast?"

I nodded. She was still in her pajamas with bed head. "Are you hungry?"

She got off the couch and ran to the kitchen. I followed her and pulled out a chair for her to climb up on. After grabbing a plate and fork for Ruth's pancakes I started a pot of coffee. Ashton would definitely be hungover and probably appreciate the gesture later.

"So did daddy ask you on a date?" I choked on the glass of water that I was drinking.

"A date?" She nodded with cheeks full of food.

I shook my head and looked down into my water. Then I heard footsteps coming down the stairs and froze. I was not expecting him to be up this early.

Ashton entered the kitchen and we locked eyes. His hair was wet and he had changed into fresh clothes after last night. Both of us were frozen with wide eyes staring at each other. Ruth looked back and forth between us like she was watching a ping pong match. "Daddy you didn't ask her?"

His face reddened and he let out a long breath. "You brought breakfast?"

I nodded and went to stand up. "No, sit I've got it. Thank you." He said quietly.

"Of course. There's coffee made too if you want it." He immediately went to pour a cup and drank from it for a long while.

He joined us at the table with his coffee mug and food. "Are you eating breakfast, Georgia?" Ruth asked.

"No, I'm not hungry." My appetite was nonexistent after last night. It wouldn't settle again until I spoke with Ashton alone.

Once they both finished their breakfast in silence Ashton got up to take what I assumed was an aspirin from a cupboard in the kitchen. He turned to Ruth and asked her if she could go get dressed on her own.

She stood up and brought her plate to the sink. "I want to wear my outer space shoes today!" And then she was upstairs in a blink.

Ashton turned to me with a solemn look on his face. "Can we talk?"

That phrase was even more damning than the fact that he confessed his love for me while drunk last night. I took a deep breath and stood up to face him. "Yeah."

He glanced upstairs and led me to the back door. He called out to Ruth. "Georgia and I are going outside for a minute. We'll be right back."

He held the door open for me and I walked past him. His arm brushed against me and I couldn't help but shiver at the contact. I walked down the steps until I was standing in the grass and turned around to look at him.

My arms crossed as I waited for him to speak first. He was the one who asked to talk so he could start this awkward conversation. My teeth gritted and I couldn't help but uncross my arms to twist one of my rings as I anxiously waited for what the hell he was going to say.

I analyzed his face and he looked just as nervous as I felt "So, I got pretty drunk last night."

Obviously. "Yeah, a little."

"I remember you driving us home and then we were sitting on the couch. And then you seemed upset and helped me in bed before leaving." He looked confused. Jesus Christ he didn't even *remember* telling me he was in love with me? That was even worse.

"Can you fill in the blanks here? Clearly I'm missing something. If you were upset I got drunk I can promise you it won't happen again. That was the first time I've been at a bar in three years so I overestimated how much I could handle." He sounded genuinely worried.

Did I really have to be the one to tell him? I debated not saying anything about it for a moment before I realized. This was Ashton. Just yesterday I was willing to do anything to tell him how I felt. And now here was this perfect opportunity to get everything out there. I could be brave just this once.

"You told me that you were in love with me. So casually, I just-" I pulled at my hair out of frustration. "I wanted to hear those words so badly but you were drunk and I didn't want to have that conversation while you were drunk."

His mouth dropped open. "Oh."

I laughed forcefully. "Yeah."

Then he stepped forward and pushed the tip of his finger under my jaw until I was looking at him. "You wanted to hear those words?"

I gulped and nodded. My heart felt like it would bust out of my chest at any second and fall between where our feet stood on the grass. "I'm so sorry I said it for the first time while drunk. I remember I couldn't stop staring and thinking about how beautiful you are. I wanted you to stay with me so I could talk to you and spend every second I could with you."

He grabbed my hands and held them both to his chest. "I'm so in love with you. Like head over heels cheesy I would do anything for you kind of love. I want to wake up next to you every morning and fall asleep holding you every night. Please."

I bit my lip to prevent a goofy smile. Tears welled up in my eyes a little, I looked away and blinked to try and convince them to go away. "Really?" I whispered. It was all I could manage without crying.

"Really, peach." He brushed a stray tear and stared at me intently.

I took a second to breathe and looked down at my feet. Willing every ounce of confidence I have, I looked back up at him. "I'm in love with you too. Like head over heels cheesy I would do anything for you kind of love."

And I was. This man pushed his way into my life and brought nothing but love and joy with him. He made me feel wanted and cared for. I had grown so much in my time living in Rosewood and it was mostly thanks to him. I was a stronger, happier person with Ashton Reid.

The smile that broke out on his face was enough to soothe every anxious feeling I'd ever had in my life. It was like taking a direct hit of serotonin. His hand slid under my jaw and wrapped around the back of my neck.

He pulled me in closer and locked his lips with mine. We kissed passionately for a full minute before he slowed and pulled away. He looked for a reaction as if he was expecting me to run again.

I grabbed his shirt. "I'm not going anywhere. I'm crazy about you Ashton Reid. These last couple of months have been the best of my life. I don't know what I would do without you and Ruth." His smile pressed up against my cheek. I was practically floating. He was happy and loved me. He was *in love* with me.

I looked up to see tears welling up in his eyes. "Don't you cry too. I'm totally going to cry now." I laughed and looked down to hide my embarrassing smile that was fully taking over my face as tears flooded into my eyes.

He laughed too and pulled me back up to look at him. He wiped my tears away and kissed both of my cheeks. I reached up to wipe away the few tears running down his cheeks too. "God, we are so sappy. This is embarrassing."

Hands went down to my thighs and lifted me up until my legs were wrapped around his waist. "This is *love,* baby. Nothing embarrassing about it." His nose nuzzled into mine as his smile continued shining.

"Daddy!" Ruth called from inside the house. Ashton sighed and leaned his forehead against mine.

"Jesus fucking Christ." He whispered with his eyes closed. He gently set my feet back on the ground before cracking the door open and yelling inside. "One minute!"

He pulled out his phone and walked back towards me. "If you need to go help her it's fi-" His finger held up to my lips stopped me.

A phone held to his ear, he silently waited. "Hey, how fast can you get here?"

I heard a muffled voice coming through the phone. Ashton responded, "Everything's fine but I want a do-over of your babysitting and I want it now."

He laughed, "Yeah, get your ass over here as fast as you can." He hung up and put his phone away.

I lifted an eyebrow. "Nick?" He smiled wickedly and moved in to give me a quick kiss.

He pulled back and walked backwards to the porch while

still smiling. "Give me twenty minutes and then you're all mine, peach."

I heard him walk inside and run up the stairs. I sat down on the porch and rested my head in my hands to take some deep breaths and calm the hell down. I was grinning like a complete moron, but Ashton Reid said he was *in love* with me.

Less than twenty minutes later Ashton came back outside and sat next to me on the porch. I looked over to see his smile. "Ruth will be with Nick for the rest of the day."

"Is that so? What ever will we do with so much alone time?" I bit my lip to hide my smirk.

He grabbed my hips and lifted me to sit on his lap before pulling my lips down to meet his. Sparks flew and my hands gripped his biceps. He pulled at my hair and his tongue pushed into my mouth at my gasp.

I pulled back to catch my breath. I took in his determined face and gave him a smile. He wrapped one arm under my ass as he stood up and moved to carry me inside. While he walked up the stairs I trailed kisses up the side of his neck and his responding groan made me smile and nip at his ear.

"Peach, you're going to be the death of me." He confessed in a low voice.

27

Georgia

As we reached the top of the stairs Ashton frantically twisted the door handle to his bedroom twice before finally being able to open the door. He walked two steps inside and slammed it shut before pushing my back up against it. His lips returned to mine forcefully and his hands slipped to squeeze my ass.

I let out a breath before he slammed his lips back down on mine.

I groaned into his mouth. He pulled back and gave me a heart melting smile. He looked so damn happy. His lips moved down to mouth at my neck before he breathed into my ear and murmured, "I've waited so long for this, peach."

My breath huffed out unevenly. "I hope you've still got those condoms."

He smiled recklessly as he walked over and threw me on his bed so hard I bounced. His movements froze for a second as he looked down at me spread out for him. Intense gaze stolen from me, he turned to his bedside table and pulled out the familiar package.

A condom was fished out and thrown onto his pillow before he grabbed at my thighs and pulled me down on the bed so he was standing between my spread thighs. He leaned down until his body hovered over me and he was held up by his arms. I looked up at him expectantly.

"What are you willing to do for it, princess?" My eyes lit up at the taunt. He was mimicking the first time we met in that grocery store.

I grinned and sat up on my elbows so he was forced to move back. I could play this familiar game. I smirked and asked slowly, "What do you want for it?"

He breathed heavily and stared at my lips. I reached for his t-shirt and played with the hem of it. His gaze fell down to my hands and he quickly moved to pull it up and over his head. The shirt was quickly forgotten on the floor as I felt his tattooed chest and traced over the tattoos leading down his abdomen.

He was mine now. Just as much as I was his. Which meant these tattoos were mine. I could look at them and touch them and feel them whenever I wanted. Ashton Reid was mine.

"I could think of quite a few things," he said against my throat. His head fell into the crook of my neck and he breathed in deeply. "I want that shampoo."

I laughed at the unexpected statement. "My shampoo? That's all you want for it?" I teased.

My hands wrapped around his abdomen to feel the muscles on his back. Ashton was made of warm cut muscle and all I wanted to do was feel him up for the rest of eternity. Then my hands wandered to the front of his shorts.

He groaned as I slipped my hand in them and gripped his

cock. He thrusted into my hand as I started moving it up and down. "Are you sure that's all you want, Ash?"

"Fuck, you are such a damn tease." He pushed my own t-shirt up and pulled down my bra to suck on my nipple. I gasped at the unexpected feeling. He pulled my hand out of his shorts and pulled my wrists together to hold over my head as he kissed me again slowly.

The tension was killing me. I felt like a rubber band stretched to its limits and could snap at any second. We played this game of cat and mouse for too damn long.

He pulled back and lifted my shirt the rest of the way off my body and threw it across the room. Hand felt around my back as I arched for him to unclasp my bra. My tits sprung free as he pulled the straps away and also threw my bra across the room.

His mouth returned to my nipple and my fingers trailed through his hair when he switched to show my other nipple some attention. He started kissing his way down my stomach to my shorts. His eyes met mine as he reached them.

His stare made me impatient. I whined, "I want them off." I moved my own hands from his hair to start unbuttoning the denim. He paused with a playful smile on his face. "*Please*."

"Anything for you princess." He finished unzipping them for me and pulled them down along with my underwear until they were nothing but a pile of clothes on the floor.

He pulled back and remained on his knees in front of me, staring again. I waited a few seconds before grabbing his hand and pulling.

He stayed still as his eyes trailed up and down my body again and again. "Ash."

Our gazes met. His voice was deep and filled with need,

"Hold on, peach. I've waited so long for this, let me just have a minute."

He continued appreciating my body as his hands came up to caress the places his eyes looked over as if he was trying to memorize my body. His fingertips slowly slid over my thighs, stomach, and up to my face to pull at my ear. Then down my arms and he pinched my nipples on his path back down my body. After minutes of what felt like torture he finally put his hands back on my thighs and pulled until my ass slid down to the edge of the bed.

Waiting until I made eye contact to continue, he then moved to kiss my inner thigh before lifting my leg up to rest over his shoulder. I squirmed as he continued his memorization between my legs. His fingers traced up my thigh and all around the one place I wanted him to touch.

"Ash, please do something. Stop teasing," I demanded. He lifted an eyebrow and pulled his mouth from where it was hovering over me.

He kissed the side of my knee and smirked. "Who knew you could be so impatient."

"*Ashton*, now." I moved to pull at his hair.

He was the one who wound me up this much. So he would damn well be the one to fix it. I looked over his strong back as his head finally tilted down and his gaze left mine.

He hummed and finally put his mouth where I wanted. I moaned loudly and arched my back. "Fuck, yes. Just like that."

His tongue flicked at my clit and my eyes shut. I couldn't stop the sounds falling from my open mouth as his tongue swirled around my clit and his fingers teased my hole. He continued to tease until I tugged at his hair again.

He slipped two fingers inside of me and I gasped. Of course

214

he was good at this. His mouth and fingers took my breath away and I lost control of my mind. All I could think was *please, please, please.* I didn't realize I was chanting it until he intertwined the fingers of his free hand with mine and squeezed.

Another finger was added and stars burst behind my eyes. "So good, Ash. Please don't stop. I'm so fucking clo-." I cut myself off with a gasp as my breath was stolen from me again. The foot hung over his shoulder dug into his back as I beckoned him closer. My entire body contracted and Ashton kept his mouth on me until I pushed his head away.

"Sensitive, fuck," I muttered. He slowly pulled back and moved my leg off of his shoulder.

He rose from his knees and stood above me. He teased, "Who knew you had such a dirty mouth, peach."

I blushed and he unbuttoned his shorts to pull them down. His eyes caught my cheeks, "I love that fucking blush. You taste almost as sweet as your cheeks look."

I bit my lip and sat up to stop him so that I could pull the shorts down myself. My nights were spent wondering what was underneath these shorts so I wanted to do the honors myself. He moved his hands and I pulled them down slowly.

His dick sprang up in my face and I breathed out a laugh. "Of course you have a big dick too."

He laughed. "Too?"

I looked back at it and slowly stroked his cock before looking back up at him through my eyelashes. "You're fucking perfect. Your smile, your acts of kindness, your body, and now your dick."

He laughed breathlessly. His eyes darkened and he offered me a hand to stand up with him. I took it and next thing

I knew my tits were pressed against his hard chest. "Jesus fucking Christ," he said quietly as he looked down at them. "You are so fucking perfect. Every inch of you."

"If you're done staring at my tits, can you fuck me now please?" I asked impatiently. Where he found the patience of a saint after we walked through that bedroom door I will never know. Just looking at his tattoos and muscles were enough to make me impatient.

He snuck his head back into the crook of my neck to leave little kisses down my shoulder. His snarky attitude was back. "I love how needy you're being."

I pouted. "How long have we waited for this again?" *Too fucking long* was the answer. I pulled back so my entire body was on display for him.

He looked me up and down once more and grabbed a handful of my ass. His words matched my thoughts exactly, "Too fucking long."

His hand went to grab the condom he left laying on the pillow. He opened the package with his teeth and quickly rolled it on his hard cock. "I've been dreaming about this, princess. Dreaming of fucking this perfect goddamn cunt."

"Lay back on the bed, baby," he demanded. I followed his orders and crawled on the bed to give him a good show of my ass. He slapped it and I squeaked before laying on my back. He quickly followed and moved his body over mine. I could feel the muscle of his thighs between mine.

His face was focused on mine and he gave me another slow kiss before continuing.

He guided his dick to slide against my clit. I mewled and my hands shot up to grip at his strong shoulders. His biceps bulged next to my head as he looked down where our bodies met. He groaned and shut his eyes while grinding into me.

"More, please." I whined. He chuckled breathlessly and moved his tip to my entrance. I cried out and my nails dug into the skin on his shoulders as he slowly pushed into me.

He paused and kissed at my neck to give me a second to adjust. I tried my best to slow my breathing and relax but his dick was fucking big. His mouth nipped at my ear when I finally relaxed, "Good girl."

Those two words alone made me moan and he chuckled. His teeth nipped the apple of my cheek next. "I love this blush. I promise to keep it on your cheeks as long as I fucking can."

He started pushing in again until his hips met mine and he was fully inside me. My entire body tensed down to my toes and he returned to his sweet kisses and nips all over my face. I counted my breaths until I adjusted to him and he breathed out.

"You okay, peach?" he whispered. I nodded and hummed.

I lifted my head until my lips met his ear. Finding my confidence I whispered, "Fuck me as hard and rough as you can. Show me what you can do Ashton Reid."

He growled as his response and lifted up my leg to rest my ankle on his shoulder. He kissed it and made eye contact before pulling out and slamming back inside of me. After the stars cleared out of my eyes I lifted my hips to meet his thrusts. His head bent down to my shoulder as he watched his cock sliding in and out of me.

I bent my head down too and nearly came at the sight. His abs flexed and I could see every muscle in his arms straining as he fucked me roughly. My head slammed back to the pillow and I squeezed my eyes shut to focus. He felt so fucking good.

"Fuck, you feel so damn good princess," he said shakily.

My mouth was hung open as he continued fucking me. The sounds flowing out of my mouth were unrestrained as I let him hear exactly how good he made me feel. His own grunts and groans spurred me on as he moaned into my neck. My leg that wasn't balancing on his shoulder came up to wrap around his waist and pull him in closer.

His head lifted to find my lips again as he kissed me slowly and passionately in time with his thrusts. I couldn't help but let my moans spill into his mouth. He smiled against my lips, "That's it, peach. I want to hear all those pretty sounds."

My hands moved down to his lower back as I arched up into him, almost reaching my high. Nails scratched up his back to pull him impossibly closer as I screamed out his name. His thrusts sped up until I came and had no sense of what was going on. All I could feel was overwhelming pleasure.

Ashton's body stiffened against mine as he pushed in hard for his last thrust. He let out one final groan into my neck as his arm moved under my back and pulled me into his chest. Once his body relaxed he breathed out and looked up at me.

I laughed airily and his dreamy smile made me return my own. "That was fucking amazing."

He laughed with me and hung his head to my chest for a second. "It was." He leaned up and trailed more sweet kisses up my neck until he met my lips.

After pulling out he gently kissed my ankle before returning my legs to the bed. I readjusted to stretch them out a bit. "Are they cramped?"

"No, just a little sore." He leaned down to kiss my calf before raising to his knees and standing up off the bed. "I'll be right back, I'm just grabbing a towel."

He turned to the bathroom and I gasped. My hand moved

218

to cover my mouth at the sight of his back. "What's wrong?" He looked terrified.

"Your back!" His head tilted before he turned to see it in the bathroom mirror. The motherfucker laughed and smiled back at me proudly.

He moved a hand behind his back to rub at some of the bright red scratch marks that trailed from the tops of his shoulders to his mid back. He snarked with a huge smile on his face, "Oh these? They're my trophy."

I rolled my eyes while he went to grab the towel and returned to wipe me up. After he was done I sat up and forced him to shift so I could see the scratch marks up close. "We need to put medicine on this. I'm so fucking sorry I didn't know I was leaving marks."

He laughed and grabbed my hand while laying down to pull me down on top of him. "We'll worry about that later." His hand moved to brush through my hair and he once again stared down at my body.

After a few minutes of silence our breathing had evened out. His hand still brushing through my hair he asked. "So would you like to go on a date with me today? Please."

I laughed and turned to face him. "Only because you asked so nicely."

He gave me a cheeky smile and flipped me onto my back again. "We still have some time to waste before that though. I can think of a few ways to keep us entertained in the meantime."

28

Ashton

Today was one of the happiest days of my entire life. And I spent ninety percent of it in bed with Georgia Mitchell. I finally got the girl and it felt better than any win I'd had on a volleyball court. We walked hand in hand into Reid's diner.

Ruth was the first to spot us and she squealed before jumping out of her seat to greet us. "You went on your date!"

I nodded and picked her up to kiss her on the cheek. "We did. It was great."

We looked over at Georgia who was blushing. I meant it when I said I would do that as often as possible. Never in my life would I grow tired of watching her cheeks turn pink. I walked her over to the table she was sitting at with Nick, Reese, and Ryan.

I put Ruth down and grabbed Georgia's hand again. We stood at the head of the table before sharing a look with heart eyes as Nick would say. I turned to my friends and proudly announced, "We're dating."

Reese gave Georgia a huge smile and high fived her. My brother raised his eyebrows at me and then smiled at Georgia. Ryan congratulated us both and Ruth grabbed both of our hands and jumped up and down with glee.

Georgia and I exchanged a glance. She was glowing again. I vowed then and there to make her the happiest I could for the rest of her life. My hand squeezed hers again before we sat down to join the rest of our friends.

Epilogue
Five Years Later
Georgia

As I tossed the comforter off of my overheated body for the twentieth time, I heard Ash sigh next to me. His hand that always found a way to touch me, even when I slept so fitfully, circled around my wrist and gently tugged on it until I shuffled closer to him and rested my head on his shoulder.

"What's wrong, peach?" He mumbled. His groggy voice sent a pang of guilt straight through my heart. The pitch black night sky and glowing red alarm clock were signs that he should definitely be sleeping.

My foot crossed over his and I snuggled in closer. "Nothing, go to sleep."

I forced myself to lie still for a few moments so he could fall back asleep. Lying on my back proved to be quite the challenge though, from the weight on top of my stomach. Discomfort quickly turned into pain and I shuffled subtly to turn to my side. Ashton's arm moved to wrap around my back as he sat up a little and brushed my hair out of my face.

"What's wrong, baby? Can't get comfy?" His voice was much

more awake now, and I knew he wouldn't go back to sleep until I gave him an explanation.

I pushed up on my elbows and joined him so we were both sitting up against the headboard while he stroked my hair. "I can just get it, it's no problem," I said after a few quiet seconds.

His hand quickly found my elbow as I moved to get off the bed. "What do you need?"

I murmured, "Your kid really wants some hot chocolate right now." My hand rubbed at my growing stomach and my head hung in mock shame.

Ashton chuckled and leaned over to kiss my forehead. "Stay still, I'll be right back."

Lying back against our bed that held far too many pillows, I nestled into one of the full length body pillows and waited patiently for my husband to return. Tomorrow would be an early morning, and getting two kids ready for a trip was no easy feat.

I woke up to a cold mug sitting on the side table in front of me and cringed at the sunlight in my eyes. Rolling over, I found Ashton passed out on his back with a forearm held over his face and his other arm lying protectively over my side. My gaze fell to the foot of our bed after hearing quiet giggles and a beam of light moving caught my eye.

Quietly sitting up with a giant bump left me a little breathless, but I managed, and found our two daughters sitting on the floor in front of our bed, playing with one of the flashlights that was supposed to be packed away for our beach house trip. Ashton was always well prepared, and even though it meant we took way too much luggage on every vacation we went on, I loved him for it.

Ruth saw I was awake first and waved at me before throwing

a blanket over her little sister's face. My eyebrow quirked and I quietly padded around the side of the bed to join them on the floor. Giggles got much louder under the blanket as I put my arms around her and pulled her into my lap while holding my stare down with Ruth.

"What exactly have you two been up to this morning?" I whispered suspiciously.

Ruth's smile displayed a gap as one of her last adult teeth was finally growing in. The sight of it made my own smile grow despite my intentions of pretending to be grumpy. With my arms held tightly around my three year old daughter in my lap, I yanked the blanket off of her head and got a good look at her face.

I couldn't help the snort that came out of my nose as I tried my best to muffle my laugh by hiding my face in her shoulder. "Ruth, why is Harper covered in stickers?"

And by covered, I meant literally every inch of her face was filled with them. Except for holes around her eyes, the stickers went up into her hairline and overlapped each other to make quite the impressive colorful masterpiece of rainbows and ponies on her face. My daughter was now ready for crime in her sticker-made ski mask.

Harper's giggles became squeals and I suspected Ash would be joining us any minute now with all of the noise. Ruth gave me a shrug and whispered, "We wanted to see how many would fit."

Suddenly, Ash swung his head over the edge of the bedframe and made all three of us jump back. He squinted at us playfully with one of my favorite smiles on his face. "Why wasn't I invited to early morning tea time?"

"Girls only," declared Ruth.

He glared at her and put a gentle hand on my stomach behind Harper's back. "Well then you've got an intruder. How come he can join, but I can't?"

"He's our brother," said Harper between giggles.

Ash reached down like a monkey and pulled Harper up into the air and onto the bed. "Yeah, and I'm your dad, you goof." He tickled her until she lost her breath from laughing and only paused to ask what the hell happened to her face.

Ruth and I decided to let him handle that and got up to head downstairs for breakfast. Now that she was almost eleven, we often made breakfast together, and because of her cooking classes with her uncle, she was usually the one in charge. I let her pull out all of the ingredients to our usual breakfast and started scrambling eggs while Ruth whipped up some pancake batter.

"Are you excited to go to the beach?" She nodded as she precisely measured a cup of flour.

"I'm glad everyone is going to be there. Although it might be a little cramped." I mumbled my agreement and fluffed up the eggs with a whisk just like she taught me to.

My whisking motions stopped as I felt a distinct kick in my side. Breathing through the slight pain, I closed my eyes for a moment before continuing to stir. When I opened them again, I found Ruth watching me.

"Is he kicking or rolling?" she asked.

"Kicking, I guess he's excited to go to the beach today too." I smiled and tried to soothe him by rubbing my stomach.

Ruth's hand surprised me as she gently pressed on the spot I was rubbing before leaning down to talk to my belly. "You be nice to mom please, she just woke up."

224

My smile widened and my heart filled with the same warmness that I felt every time Ruth called me mom. It started about a couple of years ago when Harper started talking, and it never failed to make me teary eyed. I gave my daughter a quick hug and focused on finishing breakfast before my emotion turned into full blown waterworks.

Ash and Harper loudly joined us downstairs and I leaned down to kiss Harper's sticker-free face before giving my husband a kiss good morning. He held me for a second longer than necessary while Harper got up on her stool to stand next to Ruth at the counter.

"Go, get ready. We'll make breakfast," I offered.

He nuzzled my cheek and kissed it before insisting, "You go. I've got the kids."

I sighed and grabbed both of his hands. "You're going to be insufferable today aren't you?"

"You're six months pregnant, honey, I'm not letting you pack the car." I laughed at his serious tone and headed upstairs to get ready quickly.

The table was fully set when I returned, so we all wolfed down breakfast at record speed. Reids do not mess around when it comes to breakfast.

I helped to pack the car with smaller things that Ash wouldn't throw a fit over, like snacks and pillows for our short ride to the beach.

Before Harper was born, we decided to buy a house on the shore and invite all of our family for a trip each summer. It had become tradition, and each year the house seemed to only get more and more cramped with kids and significant others.

Leaning over in my seat, I voiced those exact thoughts to Ashton as we pulled out of our driveway. "You're going to have to buy a second car if we have another kid after this one. It's cramped in here."

He laughed at me and reached over to squeeze my hand before smirking at me over his dark sunglasses. "Only one more?"

I groaned, already having an idea of what he was hinting at. "Three, *maybe* four kids is a good number." His smile only widened at my defensive tone. "How many kids do you want exactly?" I questioned.

"I think a whole volleyball team would be nice." His last word was cut off with a laugh as I pretended to put his hand back in his lap and take mine away. Quickly intertwining our fingers again he amended, "I'm happy with whatever you want baby. I've got all I need right here."

I looked out the window to try to hide my blush, but he still caught it and pretended to pinch my cheek nonetheless. Ruth leaned up from the back seat and added, "Really, daddy. The beach house is getting a little full."

"No need to worry, honeybee. Your mom here can just buy us a second one next to it with all that writing money of hers. Or we can put Uncle Nick out in the dog house. "

I scoffed and shook my head with a smile as Ruth's laugh sounded from the back seat. Harper's sweet giggles joined in the noise soon after. I just sat back and basked in the sound of my happy little family.

ACKNOWLEDGEMENT

A special thank you to my beta readers for understanding these characters and their sweet story, and taking the risk to read my debut novel. As a new author, my heart goes out to you! Thank you Lindsay, Kelly, Chelsea, and Rose.